"Remind me [never to turn?] my back on y[ou ag...]"

Hunter's voice was a harsh whisper, and just as Blair was about to yell out for help again, he pulled her to him. "No, Hunter. Don't..." Blair begged as his mouth descended on hers. No, she thought, as her lips began to soften beneath his, this can't be happening! She was melting.

Hunter gasped, suddenly pushing Blair away from him.

"Why did you do that?" Blair whispered.

"I...I...why the hell do you think?" Hunter snapped. "What you need is a gag."

Color sprang into Blair's cheeks. Of course. He'd only kissed her to silence her. "Don't ever do that again!" Blair threw back angrily.

"Don't make empty threats, Miss Desmond," Hunter said softly. "You know damned well you liked it."

God help me, Blair thought, he's right!

SANDRA MARTON says she's always believed in romance. She wrote her first love story when she was nine and fell madly in love at sixteen with the man who is her husband. Today, they live on Long Island, midway between the glitter of Manhattan and the quiet beaches of the Atlantic. Sandra is delighted to be writing the kinds of stories she loves and even happier to find that her readers enjoy them, too.

Books by Sandra Marton

HARLEQUIN PRESENTS

Don't miss any of our special offers. Write to us at the following address for information on our newest releases.

Harlequin Reader Service
901 Fuhrmann Blvd., P.O. Box 1397, Buffalo, NY 14240
Canadian address: P.O. Box 603,
Fort Erie, Ont. L2A 5X3

SANDRA MARTON

a flood of sweet fire

Harlequin Books

TORONTO • NEW YORK • LONDON
AMSTERDAM • PARIS • SYDNEY • HAMBURG
STOCKHOLM • ATHENS • TOKYO • MILAN

Harlequin Presents first edition March 1989
ISBN 0-373-11155-X

Original hardcover edition published in 1988
by Mills & Boon Limited

CHAPTER ONE

THE 747 banked gently as it dipped earthwards. Rome—the city of Caesars, the glory of a thousand-year empire—lay just below. Blair Nolan pressed her forehead to the milky porthole, trying to glimpse something through the cloud cover that had appeared along with the rising sun. It was really happening, she thought, and then the excitement faded and trepidation took its place. It was her first trip to Italy. In fact, it was her first trip anywhere, but it might be her last. It might end in a Roman prison, or wherever it was they put people who travelled on false passports.

Not false. Fraudulent. Well, perhaps not really fraudulent, but certainly illegal. The passport lying in the bottom of Blair's handbag belonged to her employer, Meryl Desmond, just as the handbag itself belonged to Meryl. For that matter, so did the clothes she was wearing. Yesterday, she'd been Meryl's personal secretary, and today—today she was Meryl Desmond, heiress to the Desmond fortune, the girl who specialised in making madcap headlines on two continents.

How did I ever let you talk me into this, Meryl?

But she knew how. The Meryl she'd come to know over the past four months was sweet and strong-willed. She'd come up with the scheme at the last minute, and talked Blair into it before she'd had time to do much thinking. She'd made it sound simple, clever and romantic. By the time Blair had realised just what she'd agreed to, it was too late.

'You can't change your mind now, Blair,' Meryl had pleaded. 'It'll be a piece of cake, you'll see. Everyone will believe you're me.'

And, so far, everyone had. The cabin attendants had all smiled and called her Miss Desmond. Even the captain had come back to greet her and wish her a pleasant flight. Of course, none of them knew Meryl personally. And none of them was a Customs inspector. None of them would look from Meryl's passport photo to Blair's face, trying to match Meryl's medium brown eyes with Blair's green-flecked ones, or Meryl's ash-brown hair with Blair's cinnamon-lit curls.

'They won't try to match anything,' Meryl had said, laughing as if sneaking on to foreign soil with someone else's passport was everyday sport. 'Besides, people never really look like their passport photos, do they? And you'll be wearing glasses like mine and bangs like mine and...'

'Yes, but...'

'If you wear my stuff and change your hairstyle, we could pass for sisters. Stop worrying. All the Customs guy will see is a good-looking woman.' Meryl had grinned mischievously. 'This is Italy you're going to, Blair, the land of *amore*. Every male past the age of puberty thinks he's Casanova.'

'Meryl, this is crazy!'

'Sure it is. Haven't you ever done anything crazy before?'

Not this crazy, Blair thought now, watching as the cloud cover parted and revealed glimpses of the eternal city. When you grew up on a farm in Iowa, the ward of an aunt and uncle who thought excitement began and ended with the annual State Fair, you didn't do much that was crazy or unusual. And even after you moved to Los Angeles, you were too busy keeping body and soul together to do anything even half-way crazy. Until

one day you answered an ad and the interviewer turned
out to be Meryl Desmond...

'Aren't we more than employer and employee, Blair?'
Meryl had said just yesterday, when Blair suddenly
balked at the thought of boarding the Alitalia plane.
'We're friends, right? And friends help each other out.'
Meryl's voice had dropped to a cajoling whisper. 'You
can carry it off. If you believe it, so will everybody else.
Just keep thinking *I'm Meryl, I'm Meryl*... It'll work,
you'll see.'

'But...but... I should never have agreed to this, Meryl.
Suppose somebody on the plane knows you? Suppose...'

'Nobody will,' Meryl had soothed. 'You're going to
have a lovely flight. First class is usually half-empty.
You'll drink champagne and eat lobster.'

'I don't like lobster,' Blair had grumped as Meryl led
her gently towards the departure lounge.

'Then you'll eat *saltimbocca alla romana*,' Meryl had
teased as she took Blair's sunglasses from her and
plopped them on her own nose. 'Relax and enjoy it,
Blair. Six hours of luxury, and then a ten-minute ride in
Daddy's limousine...'

'What about the chauffeur? He'll know I'm not you.
He...'

'He's new,' Meryl had said gently. 'He'll think you're
me, if you say you are. And before you know it, you'll
be at the villa, and then I'll be there.'

'Yes, but you...'

Meryl had grinned. 'I'll be there five minutes later—
the back of the plane lands the same time as the front.
And I'll be with Perry, and I'll explain everything to
Daddy.' Her pretty face had sobered. 'Just once in my
life, I want to do things the right way. I mean, I love
Perry, and I want Daddy to love him, too. I want him
to meet Perry without any paparazzi hanging around,
without any noise or fuss. We've escaped the photog-

raphers so far, thanks to you...' And Meryl had sighed dramatically. 'You've been wonderful, Blair. Perry and I couldn't have fallen in love without you.'

Well, Blair had thought, looking from Meryl to the man she loved, that was a bit of an exaggeration. But the two shining faces before her shattered her resolve, and finally she'd sighed and said OK, she'd give it a try. And now, here she was, accepting Meryl's Louis Vuitton carry-on bag from the flight attendant, tucking Meryl's Gucci handbag under her arm, and leaving the plane.

'*Ciao,*' the flight attendant said, and Blair smiled.

'Goodbye,' she said, and then she took a deep breath and stepped into the corridor. Signs directing the way towards Passport Control seemed to leap from the wall every few paces, and finally her footsteps slowed. A short man carrying a garment bag bigger than himself elbowed past her.

'*Scusi,*' he muttered.

Blair nodded as a woman clutching a squalling baby hurried past her, too. Go on, she thought, why don't you all get ahead of me? It's OK. But putting off the confrontation wouldn't really help. It would be just her luck to delay things long enough so that the tourist-class passengers engulfed her and she and Meryl ended up side by side, each clutching the other's passport! She had a sudden, nightmarish vision of a scowling Customs inspector looking from her employer's face to hers, trying to determine whose picture was attached to the passport that was even now becoming sweat-stained in Blair's hand.

Actually, she had to admit Meryl might be right. They did resemble each other somewhat. They were almost the same age—Meryl was just past twenty-one and Blair had just celebrated her twenty-second birthday a few months ago. Both had brown hair and brown eyes.

'We can even wear the same clothes,' Meryl had insisted. 'Haven't we borrowed each other's things?'

Yes and no, Blair thought grimly as she marched onwards. Meryl had never borrowed anything of hers. Why would she, when Meryl's clothes were custom-made and Blair's were straight off the rack? But Blair had worn Meryl's things before—once. It was right after Meryl and Perry met, and Meryl had announced they were head over heels in love and dying for some privacy. Blair had let Meryl talk her into luring the ever-present Los Angeles newshounds into following her from the house in Topanga Canyon to the glitzy stores on Rodeo Drive, so that Meryl and Perry could sneak off for a quiet afternoon at the beach.

'Thank you, thank you,' Meryl had burbled that evening. 'That's the first time in my life I ever managed to give those leeches the slip. Oh, if only I could keep things like that. I mean, if you think these Los Angeles paparazzi are bad, just wait till we get to Italy!'

And that had been the start of this whole hare-brained scheme, this disaster, this...

There it was. Customs. Blair's heart, already thudding loudly enough to sound in her ears, accelerated to a dizzying crescendo.

'What if they find out?' Blair had demanded as they had climbed into a rented limousine for the trip to the airport.

'All they'll do is wish the pretty *signorina* a pleasant stay in Rome,' Meryl had said patiently.

'Suppose they don't? Suppose they arrest me? Suppose they lock me up? Suppose...'

'I'm using your passport, Blair. And I'm not worried, am I?'

'Answer the question,' Blair had insisted.

'If anything goes wrong—which it won't—my father will send over a team of lawyers, and before you know it you'll be safe at his villa. Any other questions?'

'Yes,' Blair had sighed. 'Why do you employ a certifiable lunatic like me?'

And Meryl had smiled and ruffled Blair's new hairdo, the one that made her look like Meryl.

'You're not a lunatic,' she'd said gently. 'And I don't just employ you. You're my friend. And my companion. And a romantic.'

The line shuffled forwards. Blair's breathing quickened. No matter what Meryl said, switching identities and passports was illegal. It wasn't, Meryl had insisted. They weren't doing it so they could smuggle jewels or drugs. *That* would have been illegal. If that rationalisation had seemed flimsy back in Los Angeles, it seemed positively pathetic here. Blair could see the Customs inspector's face now, and he hardly looked the sort to believe she was anything but an impostor, and never mind these damned bangs that kept getting in her eyes and these tinted glasses that Meryl always wore and...

'*Buon giorno, signorina*. And how are you today?'

Blair swallowed as she handed over her passport. 'Fi-fine,' she said. 'Just fine.'

The man opened the blue booklet and stared at it. Blair's heart skipped erratically.

'Signorina Desmond, hmm? And are you here for business or pleasure?'

'Pl-pleasure,' Blair stuttered.

He looked up at her, his mouth unsmiling. 'And will you be staying in Roma or travelling?'

'Oh, I'll be staying in Rome,' Blair said positively. If I can just get to the Desmond villa, I'll never move out of it...

The official beamed and snapped the passport closed. *'Bene,'* he said, handing it back to her with a flourish. 'Roma is always delighted to have beautiful women visit her. Enjoy your stay with us.'

Laughter bloomed deep in Blair's chest and she fought it back. By God, Meryl had been right! There was nothing to it. It had been a piece of cake. And—now that it was over, she could admit it—it had been fun! She could hardly wait to tell Meryl how well it had gone. There was just one last hurdle, and that was nothing. She had to exit the terminal, let the photographers and reporters collect their pictures and stories, and then dive into the Desmond limousine. Unless she was lucky and there were no paparazzi waiting, but Meryl had snorted when she'd suggested that.

'Don't be silly, Blair! Of course they'll be waiting. And they'll know it's you. I mean, they'll know it's me. Oh, you know what I mean. Somebody will have passed the word. One of the flight crew, maybe. Or an airline employee—there's nothing surer than that those worms will be there. They even spy on each other.'

And there they were. The first was hurrying towards her across the terminal, cameras flying from his neck. God, it was amazing! They came out of nowhere. Meryl had warned her about it the day she'd hired her as her secretary. The paparazzi hung around the homes of celebrities, she'd said, and around places where the wealthy and the famous collected. And some of them paid for tips, which was what Meryl had been counting on.

'You're the bait,' she'd said cheerfully.

And the fish were biting, Blair thought, watching from the corner of her eye as two more paparazzi began hurrying towards her. She took a deep breath and stepped through the doors to the street outside. God, it was hot! Meryl had warned her; summer in Italy, she'd said, was like summer under a heat lamp. Blair wished she were wearing her own dark sunglasses instead of Meryl's palely tinted ones. Dark lenses would have made her feel safer. She knew it was silly, but they'd have felt like something to hide behind.

'*Signorina*—hey, Signorina Desmond, over here! Come on, give us a smile, eh? *Signorina, per favore* . . .'

The three men from the terminal had reached her side. And here came another—no, two others. Lord, the faces on those two! Scowling, unpleasant, they looked more like rejects from an American gangster film than paparazzi.

'Miss Desmond, how about a statement? Are you really just visiting your father? We heard you might be meeting somebody . . .'

There was a sudden nervous flutter in the pit of Blair's stomach. She'd never seen such determined looks before. For the first time, she realised how serious these reporters were. They might carry cameras and tape recorders, but these weren't games they were playing. They were earning their living, establishing their reputations. Meryl had told her horror stories about how far some paparazzi would go to get a picture or a story. They'd been known to chase their quarry by boat, by plane, even risk their lives—and drive the celebrities they were stalking into taking elaborate precautions to foil them.

Blair forced back the sudden urge to shake her head and tell the gathering paparazzi the whole thing was a mistake, that the woman they really wanted was somewhere behind her, probably just claiming Blair's cheap suitcase from the luggage belt. Nothing was going to happen to her. All she had to do was look for the Desmond limousine and climb into it and . . .

'Hey, *Signorina, come sta*? Smile for the camera, eh? Over here, come on, *per favore, un momento* . . .'

She was surrounded now, like a sugar cube fought over by ants. Out of the corner of her eye, she saw the two scowling men she'd noticed earlier closing in from the side. The momentary prickle of fear came again and she shook it away. Where was the limo? She could see a line of cars ahead, but not a black Mercedes with a uniformed driver.

'*Buon giorno*, Signorina Desmond. *Per piacere, una fotografia!*'

A camera loomed into her face and she pulled back from its glassy stare.

'Excuse me,' she murmured, hurrying around the woman holding it. 'Pardon me,' she said, hunching her shoulders. 'If you'd just let me...'

Dear God, she thought, it was like a bad movie! There was so much confusion, so much noise—a cacophony of voices were yelling at her in Italian and in English, and there were horns blaring everywhere. She felt as if she were choking, not just from the press of bodies, but from the smell of burning rubber and exhaust fumes. There seemed to be more traffic here than in LA, and she'd never dreamed that was possible. But the road was filled with vehicles. Small cars and big ones, taxis and motorcycles, all fighting for position.

Someone jostled her from the rear—a hand holding a microphone zoomed in and jammed into her chin.

'Tell us about yourself, *signorina*,' a voice said.

Blair pulled away from the smell of cigarettes and alcohol. Where in hell was the Mercedes? Meryl had said—ah, there it was, third in line, stuck behind a taxi being loaded with luggage, and a dusty Fiat that sat idling at the kerb. The driver's door was open; she could see the uniformed driver peering over the car and she waved frantically, knowing he was looking for her.

'Here I am!' she called. 'It's me...'

Someone jostled her again, hard, and she spun around angrily. 'Listen, will you watch that, please? I...' Her words tumbled to a halt. The two dark men from the terminal were shoving their way through the crowd of paparazzi, and there was definitely something about them that chilled her. They looked like the kind who would stop at nothing to get a story. She had no trouble imagining those two doing whatever they had to do to get an exclusive for a magazine.

'Come on,' she muttered under her breath, turning back towards the road. 'Come on...' The limo had pulled out of line and was inching past the other cars, its horn blaring, but its progress was slow. The Fiat had pulled away from the kerb, but it had stopped almost in the centre of the road, blocking everything behind it.

A hand brushed her arm, and the smell of cheap wine and garlic filled her nostrils.

'Signorina Desmond?'

The voice was a snarling whisper. Blair knew, instinctively, that it belonged to one of the dark men. She pushed away from him and ran towards the road, signalling frantically to the Mercedes.

'Here!' she called. 'I'm here...'

Suddenly, the rear door of the Fiat sprang open. Blair glimpsed a moustachioed face staring out at her, and then hands grasped her arms and began hustling her towards the Fiat's dark, yawning interior.

'Hey!' she said indignantly. 'Hey...'

'Get in the car,' an accented voice growled, and once again the odour of wine and garlic assaulted her.

'Are you crazy?' Blair said, digging her heels into the pavement. 'Let go of me!'

'Move, *signorina*, or...'

'I certainly will not,' she said. 'I...hey, stop that! Stop...'

From that moment on, everything seemed to happen with the speed of an old movie. Blair felt her feet leave the ground, and she kicked backwards as hard as she could. She heard a sharp intake of breath from the man on her left—the one who oozed bad smells from every pore—and then a startled exclamation in Italian.

'Basta,' the other man snarled, and his hand tightened on her arm until she gasped, and then, suddenly, he made a strange, gargling noise. His hand fell away from her and he crumpled to his knees. A second later, the man she'd kicked gasped and fell in a heap. And then flash-bulbs were going off in her face and people were yelling, and all at once a tall, broad-shouldered figure in a pale grey uniform was shoving the reporters away from her. The Desmond chauffeur, Blair thought giddily, and the man scooped her into his arms and hurried into the road.

'Thank you,' she gasped. 'I . . .'

Her teeth clattered together as he dumped her into the back seat of the Mercedes and slammed the door after her. She blinked and rubbed her jaw as he scrambled into the driver's seat.

'You got there just in time,' she said. 'I . . .' She fell back as the man gunned the engine. The Mercedes sprang forwards. Blair's eyes widened—the Fiat loomed ahead, blocking the road. There was a metallic crunch and a barely perceptible thud, and the Fiat spun like a top, its rear a collapsed mass of twisted metal as the Mercedes sped past it, past the terminal, racing away from the crowd that had collected. Blair peered over her shoulder as the airport receded in the distance, and then tried to swallow the dryness in her throat as she turned towards the chauffeur.

'I can't thank you enough,' she croaked, and then she laughed shakily at the sound of her own voice. 'Mer...my friends told me there were some paparazzi who would do anything to get a story, but this is ridiculous.' She took a breath and let it out slowly. 'Those men are crazy!'

She waited for the driver to answer, but he didn't. He was intent on driving, his leather-gloved hands lying alert and powerful on the steering wheel. His shoulders blocked her view of the windscreen. He was big—you could see that, even though he was seated. And he was strong. She could recall how easily he'd lifted her from the pavement. A good thing he was, she thought with a shiver. Those loonies... Would they follow her, even now? It was as if the driver had read her mind. His eyes shifted to the rear-view mirror.

'Are they coming after us?' Blair asked.

The man's eyes met hers in the mirror. They were almost the same silvery colour as his uniform, and just as devoid of emotion. He said nothing.

'I guess they got carried away in their rush for a story,' Blair said. Again, she waited for him to speak. Finally, she laughed nervously and ran her hand through her hair. 'They weren't really going to do anything, were they?'

The chauffeur's lips turned up in a cool smile. His eyes flickered over her reflection and then he looked away, intent on the road ahead. Blair glanced down at herself and flushed. Her dress had ridden up over her knees, and its top button had popped open. Quickly, her fingers trembling, she closed the button and smoothed down the skirt. She glanced up, just in time to see the man's eyes on her again.

'You—er—you hit those men awfully hard, don't you think?'

Silence. Blair ran her tongue across her lips and tried again. 'I mean, I'm sure they got what they deserved, but I wouldn't want you to be charged with anything on my account.'

He looked into the mirror again. A brief flash of something—amusement? Blair wondered—lit his eyes and then he looked away. The Mercedes was fairly flying. The car hugged the road but, even so, Blair could tell that they were moving very fast.

'Er—could we go a little slower, Mr... Mr...?'

There was no answer. You probably didn't call a chauffeur Mister, she thought, but she wasn't going to worry about the protocol of the rich and famous right now.

'What's your name?' she asked.

Still silence. Blair grimaced. Welcome to Italy, she thought. First, two crazed paparazzi were trying to do God knew what just to get a scoop, and now she was stuck in a car travelling at the speed of sound with a silent chauffeur...

Dummy! The man probably didn't speak a word of English. *This is Italy, Blair, remember? Not the good old U S of A....*

'*Scusi,*' she said in halting Italian, trying desperately to remember the few Italian phrases she'd insisted Meryl drum into her head. '*Scusi, signor. Prego, comment s'appelle...*' That was French, not Italian. *Como se llamo?* No, no, that was Spanish. She took a breath and tried again. '*Signor, come si chiama?*' That was it! '*Io non parlo Italiano. Io...* Oh, God, I wish you spoke English!'

The silver-grey eyes met hers. 'I speak it impeccably,' he said.

Blair let out a sigh of relief at the sound of his American accent. 'Thank heavens,' she said, falling back against the seat. 'For a minute I thought... Thanks very much. You saved my life back there.'

She smiled into the rear-view mirror as his eyes met hers again, but his expression, what little she could see of it, remained impassive.

'No problem,' he said finally.

'Well, I... I just wanted to thank you. I... What do I call you? I mean, you must have a name.' For some reason she couldn't determine, she laughed nervously.

'Hunter.'

His voice was flat, the intonation cold. Blair swallowed drily. She had little experience with servants and none with chauffeurs—back in LA, Meryl drove her own fire-engine red Corvette—but this man certainly didn't seem to be going out of his way to be pleasant. Not that he had to be. All he had to be was competent, and he seemed to be that, she thought. The Mercedes was moving along rapidly, passing other cars with ease. A ten-minute trip to the villa, Meryl had said. Then they were probably almost there. Thank goodness. It would be very nice to go back to being Blair Nolan again. It would be wonderful, in fact. It would be...

A ten-minute trip? Blair glanced at her watch. She was still on New York time—it had been confusing enough to gain three hours during the five-hour flight from Los Angeles to New York, without gaining six hours more in the time difference between New York and Rome, and so she'd decided to wait before resetting her watch again. But the passage of minutes was still the same. The plane had touched down at ten minutes after the hour. She'd left thirty-five minutes later—she'd noticed the big clock as she hurried through the terminal—and even allowing for all the confusion after that, not more than another twenty minutes could have elapsed. But her watch showed that almost forty minutes had gone by. How long had the Mercedes been eating up the road? A long time, she thought, and a chill feathered along her spine. Certainly a lot longer than ten minutes.

She had a sudden, awful thought. Lord, how embarrassing if...

'Ex-excuse me,' she said, clearing her throat and sitting forwards on the seat. 'I... I just wondered...' She laughed nervously. 'This *is* the Desmond car, isn't it?'

The driver glanced into the mirror. His lips parted, drawing back from even, white teeth in a smile that chilled Blair's bones.

'You *are* Meryl Desmond, aren't you?' he asked softly.

She would for ever remember her brief hesitation. Tell him no, she thought suddenly, tell him you're not, tell him... But that was silly. She had agreed to be Meryl Desmond until she reached the villa. The hard part was over; this was the easy stuff. Blair smiled into the mirror.

'Yes,' she said finally, 'of course I am.'

His voice was a silken whisper. 'In that case,' he said, 'this is the Desmond car.'

CHAPTER TWO

IF YOU'RE Meryl Desmond, then this is the Desmond car.
That was what he'd said. It was what she'd wanted to
hear—wasn't it? Then why did she have this sudden
hollow feeling in the pit of her stomach? There was
something strangely chilling in his soft, almost mocking
tone. Blair looked up quickly, seeking Hunter's reflection in the mirror, but his concentration seemed
centred on the narrow road, which had turned into a
twisting track that spiralled upwards.

Her imagination was working overtime, she thought,
shaking her head impatiently. There was nothing wrong
with what he'd said. His reply to her question had been
a bit insolent. No, not insolent, exactly. Arrogant. Yes,
that was the word. Arrogant. That was the way he'd
behaved from the start. Not that his attitude was her
problem, of course. Still, she'd tell Mr Desmond that
the muscle-bound guy in the silver suit was hardly
chauffeur material.

'Are we almost there?' she asked suddenly, her voice
unnaturally loud in the silence.

'Almost.'

A single word this time, but that damned touch of
insolence was in his tone. Her eyes flashed to the mirror.
Meryl Desmond wouldn't let him get away with this kind
of nonsense. Well, it was time to show Mr Hunter who
was in charge here.

'What does "almost" mean, Hunter? Five minutes?
Ten? Half an hour?'

'Twenty minutes or so, Miss Desmond.'

Blair nodded. 'Thank you,' she said crisply.

'You're welcome,' he answered silkily, and then his eyes slid from hers.

Damn the man! Did he always have to have the last word? Did it always have to sound vaguely menacing? There was something strange about him, something...something threatening. Yes, that was the word for Hunter. There was a hint of violence in him, in the way he spoke, the way he smiled, even the way he moved. Blair's eyes focused on his back, on the play of muscle beneath the grey jacket, on the way his shoulders stretched the fabric. She could still remember the ease with which he'd swung her into his arms at the airport, the solid feel of muscle beneath her hands as she'd clung to him. Her glance moved to his thick, dark hair and the way it curled silkily over the stiff, stand-up uniform collar. Didn't chauffeurs wear caps?

Suddenly, it seemed important to see Hunter's face. Strange, she thought, they'd been in this damned car over an hour, she was sure of that, but she still didn't know what he looked like. His eyes were that strange silver-grey colour, his nose was narrow and his mouth a hard, thin line—but she had no idea how all those things looked together, although she suspected that if she could manage to put them in the perspective of a face, the man driving this damned car to God only knew where was good-looking.

He certainly wasn't your usual chauffeur, she thought, and then she shook her head. What was that supposed to mean? She didn't know a damned thing about what chauffeurs were supposed to look like. Besides, that was silly. Chauffeurs were people, that was all. They looked like anybody else and they drove cars for a living, although somehow she couldn't picture the man at the wheel of the Mercedes driving Meryl's father from place to place, waiting patiently outside one of the Desmond factories or offices.

Her pulse quickened. Stop that nonsense! What else is he if not a chauffeur? Her imagination was taking over again. Well, why wouldn't it? She'd been all keyed-up ever since they'd left the States. And she hadn't slept a wink during the flight. Jet lag, that was it. What she needed was a hot bath and a long nap, and surely she'd have both any minute now. Blair took a breath and leaned forwards.

'Mr Hunter?' He looked into the mirror and she smiled politely. 'Aren't we going awfully fast?'

'Mr Hunter?' he repeated. 'Are you always so formal with your servants?'

She flushed. 'Are you always so rude?'

'Forgive me, Miss Desmond.'

His tone made a mockery of the apology. For an instant, she was tempted to tell him he was wasting his insults if he thought he was heaping them on his employer's daughter, but then she changed her mind. A man like this would probably be even ruder to her if he knew she was an impostor. Let the Desmonds worry about their new chauffeur's behaviour.

'I take it there's been a change of plans,' she said calmly. 'I mean—we're not going to the villa, is that right?'

'Quite right.'

She waited for him to say something more. Finally, she looked into the mirror. He was looking at it, too, but his eyes were focused beyond hers.

'Would you mind telling me where we're going?' she asked impatiently.

'Somewhere safe.'

What was that supposed to mean? 'Where, exactly?'

'Outside Rome.'

Blair clicked her tongue. 'I can tell we're outside Rome...'

'Clever girl,' he said softly.

'And I don't like your tone, Mr Hunter,' she said angrily. 'I intend to tell Mr...to tell my father that you're insolent.'

He grinned. "You mean, I'm not what he told you to expect?"

He was new to the job, Meryl had said. Well, she thought grimly, he wouldn't be the Desmond chauffeur very long, not if she had anything to do with it.

'I expect to be treated with courtesy and respect,' Blair said curtly. 'When I tell him how you behaved...'

His harsh laughter cut her off in mid-sentence. 'You're scaring the wits out of me, Miss Desmond. I'm positively terrified.'

Something was very wrong here. Blair took a deep breath.

'You haven't answered my question,' she said. 'I asked you where we were going.'

'Look, just make yourself comfortable, OK? I haven't got time to do a travelogue.'

The artificially chilled air inside the Mercedes suddenly seemed frigid. 'Hunter,' she said, hoping he couldn't hear the fear in her voice, 'I want to know where you're taking me. I demand...'

Blair gasped as the car shot forwards. 'Shut up and put your seat-belt on,' he said, staring past her in the mirror.

'Don't you dare give me orders, Hunter! I asked you a question...'

'Put the belt on, Miss Desmond. If you make me stop and do it for you, you'll regret it.'

Her heart banged against her ribs as she fumbled with the belt buckle. Was he crazy? The car was still picking up speed, rocking from side to side as it ate up the narrow road. Hunter was bent forwards over the steering wheel, glancing occasionally into the mirror, his mouth grim. The taste of fear, copper-sharp and acidic, filled Blair's mouth. OK, she thought, OK, it's time to face facts. She was trapped in a car with a crazy man. She looked into the mirror and then she reached out carefully and touched the doorhandle.

And then what? For starters, the door was probably locked electronically. Expensive cars had all kinds of electronic gadgets. Even she knew that. And if it weren't, what next? Only a fool would jump out of a car speeding along the way this one was. She was scared, she thought, but she wasn't stupid...

Play it cool, Blair. Act as if you're in command here. Take a deep breath. Good. Now, take another...

'OK,' she said firmly, 'that's enough. I demand that you stop this car at once.' There was no answer. Blair leaned forwards as far as the seat-belt would permit. 'Did you hear me?' she demanded. 'I told you to stop this car. I...'

Hunter glanced into the mirror, his eyes icy and dismissive.

'Shut up.'

'Listen, Hunter, I don't know who the hell you think you are, but...'

'I haven't got the time for this, Miss Desmond. Just sit back and keep quiet.'

'I will *not* keep quiet! And you're to slow down, do you hear? This second. This...'

'Dammit to hell, Desmond,' he snarled, 'shut up or I'll...'

The unspoken threat hung in the air between them. Blair's eyes widened, and she sank back against the leather seat. Nothing made sense. Unless... a paparazzi after an exclusive story? Meryl had told her Italian reporters did crazy things, but this was insane! Nobody would... Her mind refused to accept the word. Nobody would kidnap Meryl Desmond for a story...

'No!'

The whispered cry was torn from her throat. No, it couldn't be. It couldn't! But suddenly Meryl's voice was in her head, as clearly as if they were seated next to each other.

'I love Italy,' Meryl had said when they were packing. 'The people, the food, the climate—the only thing is, I won't have the freedom I have here in the States.'

'Because of the paparazzi, you mean,' Blair had said, and Meryl had sighed.

'I wasn't thinking of them. There have been some abductions in Italy, Blair. You must have read about it in the papers. Kidnapping for ransom. Daddy's always worried about it, and especially this summer, with labour troubles at his mills—well, I'll just have to get used to not straying from the villa without an escort.'

Oh, God, Blair thought, staring at the dark head before her. No, please...

The car slid around another curve and she fell sideways, banging her elbow against the door.

Hunter must have heard the thud. He looked into the mirror; his eyes locked with hers and the breath caught in her throat. The look of cool amusement and insolence had been replaced by one of ruthless calculation.

'So you finally figured it out, did you? Why the surprise, Miss Desmond? You've always known this might happen.'

'But...'

'Just relax and take it nice and easy,' he said softly. 'It won't help to get upset.'

Her head fell back against the seat. That was it, then. She'd not only fooled a flight crew and a Customs official and a crowd of reporters, she'd fooled a criminal into thinking she was Meryl Desmond. The famous Meryl Desmond. The rich Meryl Desmond. The...

The Mercedes began to slow. What was the matter with her? Had the game of switched identities muddled her brain? Blair almost laughed aloud with relief. All she had to do was tell this man the truth. She was Blair Nolan from Iowa, and the closest she ever came to the Desmond millions was when she cashed her pay cheque.

'You...' The word came out as a croak. She swallowed and began again. 'You're making a terrible mistake.'

Hunter glanced into the mirror. 'No mistake.'

'But you are, Mr Hunter. I'm not who you think I am. I'm not Meryl Desmond.'

He laughed. It was a short, harsh sound, and it made her heart shrink icily.

'Right. And I'm Mother Goose.'

'But I'm not. Really. I swear, I'm not Meryl Desmond...'

His eyes sought hers again. She could see the sudden narrowing of his mouth, the tensing of a muscle in his jaw.

'Aren't you?' he asked in a soft whisper.

She shook her head. 'No, I'm not. Of course I'm not. I...'

But, if she wasn't the Desmond heiress, what would he want with her? She'd be useless to him. She'd be a liability, a living, breathing witness to his criminal act...

And he'd have to dispose of her. The air seemed to rush from her lungs. God, he'd kill her! She had no doubts about it. Just look at what he'd already done. He'd clobbered those poor paparazzi, he'd carried her off—she didn't even want to think about what he must have done to the real Desmond chauffeur to get this uniform and car.

The air seemed suddenly unbreathable. Blair took a shallow breath and then another. He was watching her;

she could sense it. She looked up slowly through her lashes, trying to prepare herself for the second their eyes would meet. Finally, his silver gaze caught hers.

'So,' he asked softly, 'are you Meryl Desmond?'

Blair nodded. This time, she knew what her answer had to be. 'Yes,' she said quickly, 'of course I am.'

Hunter bared his teeth in a quick smile. 'Of course you are,' he said, his tone of voice almost conversational. 'Who else would you be?'

They had slowed now, almost to a crawl. The car was travelling along a ridge on a stretch of dirt that seemed more a cart track then a road. Straggly pines and cypresses dotted the hillside; she could see a scattering of houses and the spire of a church in the valley far below. Blair had no idea where they were. It could have been ten miles outside Rome or a hundred. For all she knew, they might have spent the last hour driving in circles. The only certainty was that she was far from home and very much alone.

The Mercedes swung sharply to the right, the engine labouring softly as they climbed towards a stand of cypresses at the top of a gentle rise. She caught a glimpse of a small, white villa, and then the trees seemed to swallow them up. An outbuilding stood at the end of the little grove and, as they approached, Hunter pressed something on the dashboard. There was an electronic whine and the door ahead slid slowly upwards. The car slipped into the narrow interior and the door whispered shut behind them. The muted sound of the engine died and silence surrounded them.

He turned in his seat and looked at her. 'We're here,' he said.

Where? she wanted to ask, but she knew it was useless to do so. He'd no more answer that question than any of the others she'd asked. She nodded and ran her tongue over her lips.

'What ... what now?'

'Now we get out of the car,' he said, sounding as if she were a five-year-old, 'and we go into the house.'

The thought of being locked inside the stone walls of the villa with him terrified her. At least, on the road, there had been some chance of escape, no matter how slim. She shook her head and curled her fingers around the edge of the seat. Suddenly, the car seemed a safe haven.

'No,' she whispered.

'Yes. You'll find the door is unlocked now, Miss Desmond.'

Dimly, her brain registered that she'd been right about the door lock. But that didn't matter. What mattered was what was going to happen next.

'Listen,' she said quickly. 'I don't think ...'

In one impatient motion, he stepped out of the car and wrenched the rear door open.

'That's a good idea,' he growled. 'Don't think. Just do as you're told.' She gasped as he reached towards her. His arm brushed against her breast, the heat of it searing her flesh through her thin cotton dress.

'Don't!' she gasped. 'Please ...'

But he was already touching her, his fingers flying impatiently across the seat-belt as he unbuckled it. His hand brushed her belly, and she drew in her breath, as if to minimise the contact.

'You're making a mistake ...'

'When I want your advice, I'll ask for it,' he said. 'Get out.' Blair shook her head. Hunter cursed under his breath and his hand curled around her wrist. In one quick move, he pulled her from the car, then reached past her and snatched up the Vuitton carry-on. 'All right,' he muttered, 'let's go.'

'Mr Hunter, won't you listen to me? This isn't necessary. I...'

'I'll be the judge of what's necessary, Miss Desmond.
Now, get moving.'

'You're making a mistake. You...'

Blair cried out as Hunter's arms closed around her.
For the second time that day, he lifted her against him
as easily as if she were weightless.

'Don't you ever keep quiet, woman?' he demanded as
he stalked towards the rear garage door.

He grunted as he set her down on her feet, his left
arm tightening around her as he reached for the
doorknob with his right hand. Blair's face pressed into
his shoulder, her nostrils filled with the combined scents
of sun and fresh air and the man himself, and then he
swung her into his arms again and stepped out into the
hot sunlight. The villa she'd glimpsed through the trees
loomed ahead and Blair's heart began to race.

'Please,' she whispered, 'take me back to Rome.'

Hunter laughed, and his arms tightened around her.
'Not on your life!'

Blair closed her eyes. The whole world seemed to be
waiting for her next move. There was total silence, except
for the thud of Hunter's heart beneath her ear and the
buzz of the cicadas. And then, suddenly, she heard the
drone of a labouring engine. A car was coming! Her
pulse began to race. If she could just get the driver's
attention...

'Help!' she yelled. 'Hel——'

'You damned little...' Hunter's mouth cut off her
desperate cry. Blair gasped as his lips took hers, as his
hand caught the nape of her neck and held her head
immobile beneath the bruising onslaught of his mouth.
She felt the fluttering wings of terror beat in her veins—
and then, to her horror, something else stirred deep

within her, some dark, primeval thing without form or dimension. Hunter made a sound deep in his throat; his arms clasped her so tightly she was sure her bones would snap. For the space of a heartbeat, her mouth trembled beneath his. And then sanity returned and Blair's hands became fists that beat against her captor's chest.

She gasped for breath as the door to the villa opened and then closed behind them.

'Damn you,' she whispered, 'damn you...'

He laughed as he deposited Blair on the floor. 'Undoubtedly,' he said.

'You can't do this,' she said. 'This is the twentieth century.'

Her eyes widened. Hunter was still laughing, his silvery eyes locked with hers. His fingers reached for the top button of his uniform jacket.

'Not in these hills, it isn't,' he said softly.

She watched in disbelief as he unbuttoned the form-fitting jacket and shrugged it from his shoulders. Beneath it, his chest was naked. Blair's eyes skimmed across the well muscled shoulders and biceps, along the covering of dark, fine hair that tapered to a narrow line as it disappeared beneath his waistband.

'No,' she begged, backing away from him, 'please don't.'

But he was already unbuttoning his trousers, unzipping them, kicking off his shoes, until finally he stood before her, wearing only a pair of dark blue briefs that left little to the imagination as they clung to his hips. Unwillingly, Blair looked at him and then dropped her gaze lower, down the length of his thighs and muscled legs, then swept it back to his face.

'Mr Hunter,' she said, 'I... I...'

His teeth drew back from his lips in a quick, cold smile. 'Now it's your turn, Miss Desmond,' he said softly.

'My...' It was impossible to speak. Terror had made her mute.

Hunter nodded. When he spoke, his voice was like silk. 'Take off your clothes, Meryl,' he whispered. 'Strip.'

CHAPTER THREE

COURAGE came to her from somewhere, perhaps from desperation. If Hunter was going to rape her, she'd be damned if she'd make it easy! Blair took a breath and lifted her chin.

'No,' she said, the word faint, papery, but firm.

His eyebrows drew together in a scowl. 'You have a short memory, Meryl. I said you were to do as you were told.'

'I'm not taking my clothes off,' she said.

He tilted his head to the side and looked at her. 'Don't argue with me. I'm not a patient man under the best of circumstances.'

'I am not getting undressed,' she repeated, amazed at how steady her voice sounded, when her heart was beating so rapidly she knew it would surely leap from her breast any second.

Hunter looked at her speculatively and then he shrugged his shoulders. 'Have it your own way,' he said, almost casually. 'I though we'd do this the easy way, but it's up to you.'

He took a step towards her, his face expressionless. Blair's hands knotted at her sides. 'I'll kill you if you touch me,' she whispered.

He stared at her, and then he threw back his head and laughed. 'With what? Those hands that have never done an honest day's work? Come on!' The laughter died as quickly as it had begun, and his head dropped forwards. 'Now stop stalling and do it.'

She stumbled backwards, her eyes unflinchingly locked with his. This was it, then, she thought, and in the last minutes before her life changed for ever, she was suddenly desperate to at least recover her own name.

'Not Meryl,' she blurted. 'Blair.'

It stopped Hunter's relentless stalk and his eyes narrowed. 'What the hell does that mean?' he growled.

How could she have been so stupid? How could she have forgotten that rape, as terrible as it was, wasn't all she had to fear from this man?

'I... I meant that no one calls me Meryl.'

'Don't give me that,' he said, his face dark with suspicion. 'Your father calls you Meryl. The papers call you Meryl. That's your name, isn't it?'

She felt the cold trickle of sweat down her back. 'I... My friends call me Blair. Blair's my middle name—a family name. I... I took it when I was twenty-one...'

She held her breath while Hunter stared at her, and then he nodded. 'Yeah, it figures. Meryl's too solid a name for a girl like you, isn't it?'

Blair thought of the great-grandfather for whom she'd been named, the stodgy progenitor of the Iowa Nolans. 'I guess,' she said softly.

'OK, Blair, have it your way. Frankly, I don't care what you call yourself, just as long as you get your clothes off.'

'No,' she said again.

His eyes swept over her slowly and he sighed. 'We do it the hard way, then.'

Her shoulders hit the wall as she took a final step backwards. 'Don't,' she said, slapping at Hunter's hands as he reached for the top button on her dress.

His fingers closed around her wrists and he drew her hands down. 'Behave yourself, dammit!' he growled. 'I don't have time for this nonsense.'

She twisted her head to the side, trying to pull away from him, but her strength was no match for his. His breath fanned her face as the tiny buttons on her cotton dress came open, one after another. She felt his fingers graze her flesh, their calloused tips heated against her skin. Fear knotted inside her and she began to struggle in earnest. Hunter cursed softly and dragged her wrists above her head; his free hand encircled her throat and held her still against the wall.

'I'm warning you,' he said softly, 'don't fight me. Don't...'

She twisted her body to the side and brought her knee up between them, aiming for his vulnerable centre, but he was too quick. His body slammed against hers, driving the breath from her as he pinned her to the wall.

'You little fool!' he snarled. 'You're asking for trouble—and I'm the one to give it to you. I...'

Blair whimpered softly as she suddenly realised how foolish she'd been. One second he was restraining her, pinioning her beneath him and the next—the next his eyes were darkening to quicksilver and his body was hardening against hers. She felt her strength draining away and she slumped against the wall, eyes closed, willing it to at least be quick—but suddenly Hunter's hands dropped to his sides and he stepped away from her. Her eyes snapped open in stunned surprise.

'We're losing time,' he rasped, turning away and running his hands through his dark hair. 'Get out of that damned dress and into something else.'

The only sound in the room was the rasp of his breath. She clutched the open neckline of her dress together as she stared at him and tried to make sense out of what had happened, and then he spun towards her and kicked the carry-on across the floor.

'Let's go,' he barked. 'Hurry!'

'You mean... you mean you want me to change my clothing?' she breathed.

'Put on something easier to move around in,' he said over his shoulder as he stalked across the room. 'Or have you only got rich-girl outfits in that bag of yours?'

She watched, bewildered, while he yanked open a wardrobe and pulled men's clothing from it.

'I... I'm not sure,' she said finally. 'I mean, I don't remember...'

What had Meryl tucked into the Vuitton bag? Toiletries. A nightgown. What else?

'We'll put my usual into the carry-on in case somebody looks,' Meryl had said. 'I never carry much—just a change of clothing in case the plane's delayed. As for the rest, it's easier to just keep a wardrobe at each house, you know?'

'I... I think I have a pair of trousers and a sweater,' Blair said hesitantly, watching as Hunter slipped into khaki trousers. 'Is that all right?'

'That's fine,' he said in clipped tones. He pulled a black cotton sweater over his head. 'And do something with your hair.'

She put her hand to her head. 'My hair?'

'Jesus, don't you understand English? Yes, your hair. Pull the bangs back, tie it at the nape of your neck, I don't care. Just so long as you look different. And be quick about it.' He sank down on the edge of a chair and began to pull on a pair of sneakers.

He wanted them to change their appearance, she thought, unzipping the carry-on. The police would have been alerted by now; they'd be watching for a man in a chauffeur's uniform and a girl dressed as she was. Did that mean they weren't staying here, then? Hope filled her.

'Are... are we going somewhere else?'

Hunter looked up. 'Give the lady ten points,' he said unpleasantly. 'Come on, get a move on.'

The colour rose in her cheeks. 'Not with you here,' she said quietly.

She'd made the remark without thought and, as soon as the words were out, she held her breath, waiting for his reaction, wondering if she'd pushed him too far. She thought at first she had. His eyes narrowed, his mouth hardened, and then, to her surprise, he laughed again.

'You're full of surprises, aren't you, Meryl Blair Desmond? All right, I'll turn my back.'

'I want you to leave the room.'

'I can always go back to the first plan,' he said softly. 'I can undress you myself and...'

She pulled Meryl's clothing from the carry-on. 'Turn around,' she said stiffly.

He stared at her for a long moment and then he turned away slowly, standing with his hands on his hips.

'Make it fast,' he said gruffly.

Her hands trembled as she unbuttoned the dress and opened her belt. The dress slipped from her body, puddling in a soft heap around her feet.

'Are you ready?'

Her head sprang up at the impatient sound of his voice. 'No,' she said, zipping up the white trousers. 'Just give me a minute...'

'Ready or not,' he said softly, that hint of repressed violence in his voice again.

Blair tugged the sweater down just as he swung around to face her. His silver-grey eyes were flat as pewter as they swept over her with disinterested appraisal, lingering on the rapid rise and fall of her breasts beneath the thin sweater. When he walked towards her, she drew in her breath.

'Your hair,' he said. 'I told you to do something with it.'

She flinched as he reached his hand out towards her, but he only tucked her shoulder-length hair behind her ears. 'Better,' he said, and then he combed his fingers through the wispy bangs, drawing them back from her forehead. His hands cupped her face and finally he nodded. 'OK, that should do it. Let's go.'

They *were* leaving, then. Blair felt weak with relief. He could change the way they looked, she thought as he grasped her arm and hurried her through the villa, but he couldn't change the looks of the car. The Mercedes was big and distinctive. He might change its licence plates—she'd seen that in the movies often enough—but the luxurious car would still stand out on these narrow country roads. It...

She stumbled to a halt as the rear door of the villa slammed shut behind them.

'No,' she said, staring at the sleek silver Lamborghini drawn up snugly against the rear wall.

Hunter barely glanced at her as he unlocked the passenger door. 'What's the matter, Miss Desmond? Don't you like it?'

She swallowed drily. 'What about the Mercedes?'

'Get in.'

She did as he ordered, watching as he walked to the driver's side and slipped into the car.

'I... I thought we'd use the limousine...'

The car roared to life. 'Sorry, Blair,' Hunter said, gunning the powerful engine, 'you'll have to ride up front with the hired help.'

Her hopes of rescue faded as the Lamborghini skidded on to the road. An Italian car on an Italian road—no one would ever notice them now.

It was as if he'd read her thoughts. 'Sit back and relax, sweetheart,' he said in mocking tones. 'From here on in, we're just two people out for a Saturday drive.'

At first she sat stiffly erect, watching for a chance to get away or to signal for help. But Hunter had, once again, insisted she wear her seat-belt.

'Your father wouldn't want his little girl to get hurt,' he'd taunted when she'd chosen to ignore his command, and she'd had to suffer the indignity of sitting still beneath his quick-moving hands while he buckled her in.

And the doors on the Lamborghini locked automatically, too. He'd made a special point of showing her that. After a while, she felt herself sag back into the bucket seat. There was no point in sitting straight as a ramrod, looking for an escape route that didn't exist. The miles and the hours passed in a blur and Blair felt herself falling into a kind of stupor. The car fairly flew over the dusty Italian roads; under other circumstances, she would have been delighted by the handsome countryside. The road they were on was narrow. It curved along low, umber-coloured hills and between fields lush with early summer harvest. They passed farmhouses standing stolidly beside the road, looking as if the centuries had left them untouched.

When they approached a village, Hunter changed into a lower gear, slowing the car as it entered the narrow, cobbled streets. An old woman, dressed all in black, stared at them suspiciously. Outside a small *osteria,* men in shiny black suits looked up from glasses of dark red wine, their faces blank. It was impossible for Blair to imagine any of them coming to her assistance, even if she could make them understand that she needed help. All she could do was sit back in her seat, try to ignore Hunter's close proximity, and wait for the right moment. It was the one hope she had.

She glanced at him as the car began to speed away from the village. His face, seen in profile, was impassive. His hands lay loosely on the steering wheel. They were strong hands, encased in leather driving gloves, the fingers long and lean. He gave the impression of a man ready for almost anything, she thought, watching the flex of muscle beneath his dark cotton sweater. Suddenly, she remembered the feel of his arms around her, the hard power of his body pressed against her. A dizzying wave of heat rose within her and she tore her eyes from him and stared out the window.

What kind of man chose to be a criminal? Hunter was intelligent, at least he seemed to be. He wasn't conventionally handsome—he was too rugged-looking for that—but he was the sort she was sure most women would have found appealing. He had a strong, square jaw, high cheekbones, dark, thick lashes. Under other circumstances, even she...

Whose villa had they stopped at when they changed clothing and cars? she wondered. There had been little time to look around; all she'd had the chance to notice was that it was sparsely, if handsomely, furnished. There had been no touches to indicate what kind of person owned it, nothing but the clothing in the wardrobe. Was it Hunter's villa? It had to have been, she thought, glancing at his unyielding profile. But why would an American live in the middle of nowhere? Why would he live in Italy, for that matter? Unless the villa was rented, unless he was here for only this purpose—to kidnap her, to hold her for ransom.

Correction, Blair reminded herself. He'd kidnapped Meryl, or at least he thought he had. And, if she wanted to stay healthy, he had to keep believing it until he made his ransom demands. He hadn't, yet, not unless he had an accomplice who'd contacted the Desmonds. And once that happened, things would begin to move more quickly. Meryl's father would, she was sure, go along with the pretence that the kidnappers had snatched the right woman. Oscar Desmond would realise, as she had, that her very life depended on it. How much would Hunter demand for her safe return? Thousands? Or millions? After all, there was no limit to what such a wealthy man would be willing to pay to get his daughter back...

'Oh, God...' The cry of anguish broke from her before she could stop it. Blair caught her bottom lip between her teeth, but it was too late. Hunter had heard the whispered words.

'What is it?' he demanded.

She shook her head. 'Noth—nothing.'

He looked at her again. 'Are you ill?'

'No, no, I'm fine.'

'Then what was that sound?'

'I... I have a headache,' she lied. 'That's all.'

Hunter frowned, but finally he turned back to the road. Blair let out her breath and lay her head back against the seat. How could she have been so stupid? All these hours, she'd been careful to let her abductor think she was Meryl Desmond, telling herself that by doing so she was guaranteeing her safety. Now, suddenly, the truth had loomed before her. What would happen when Hunter or whomever he was working with finally made his ransom demand? Everything would fall apart, that's what would happen. Meryl's father would have paid whatever was asked to get his daughter returned safely. But she wasn't his daughter, she was Blair Nolan, for God's sake, his daughter's secretary, and she'd only been that for a few short months...

Don't think about it, Blair told herself. Don't look ahead. Just play along, do what you must do, get from moment to moment and hour to hour...

Her eyes flew open as the car swung sharply across the road. 'What's the matter?'

'You weren't just pretending that you don't speak Italian?'

She frowned at the cryptic question. 'No. Why do you ask?'

He nodded, as if she'd said something that pleased him. 'Good. In that case, we're stopping for coffee.'

Blair's mouth gaped open. 'We're doing what?'

He pulled up in front of an old building and shut off the engine. 'You look like hell,' he said shortly.

Her eyes narrowed. 'I'm sorry if I'm not the girl of your dreams, Mr Hunter.'

'And you're even more charming than usual,' he added drily. 'Maybe you need a break.'

'Are you serious?' she asked warily, staring at the weathered sign hanging from the building. *Caffè*, it read. *Dolce. Pane. Glacè*.

'It isn't the kind of place you're used to,' he said, getting out of the car, 'but it's the best I can do on such short notice.'

Blair stepped from the Lamborghini hesitantly, half expecting some trick. Hunter took her by the wrist as she stood up.

'I ... aren't you af ...'

She regretted the question immediately, but it was too late. Hunter smiled coldly.

'Give me credit for some intelligence, Blair. I've been watching the road for hours. No one's following us. And I don't want to disappoint you, but I'll bet my life that no one in this little town's ever heard of you. Come on, let's go. Just remember to behave yourself.'

She nodded as he took her arm. His stride was long; she was almost running in her efforts to keep up with him. Her heart pounded in anticipation. Hunter could say what he liked; the news must have gone out by now. Someone might recognise them.

He pushed open the door and they stepped inside a dark, smoky room, pungent with the scents of olive oil and wine. There was a short counter at one end, with a couple of stools before it. Two round, stained tables stood near the door. At their entrance, the handful of men in the room became silent. Gnarled faces turned towards them.

'*Buon giorno,*' Hunter said, sliding his arm around her waist. She stiffened as his fingers spread on her hip, their pressure a warning. '*Posso comprare due caffè, per piacere?*'

Blair understood nothing but the word for coffee. At first, she thought no one else had understood him, either, for no one moved. And then a small woman wearing a white apron bustled towards them.

'*Si, si, signor. Due caffè. Sedersi,*' she added, gesturing to one of the little tables.

Hunter smiled. '*Grazie, signora. E anche un dolce per la signorina, si?*'

'*Ah, si, si. Un momento.*'

'Sit down,' he muttered quietly as the woman scurried off. 'No, not opposite me—next to me, at this table.'

Blair slid into a rickety chair. 'Did you say something to her about me? I heard you say *signorina*.'

He shrugged. 'I asked her to bring you a sweet.'

She stared at him. 'Why?'

'What do you mean, why? Because you said you had a headache, and I thought maybe it was because you were hungry. Jesus, are you always so damned suspicious?'

'Are you trying to be funny, Mr Hunter?'

'There you go again,' he said. 'You question every damned thing I say, do you know that?'

'And you find that surprising?' Blair looked at him in disbelief. 'I suppose you'd like me to...to trust you.'

His eyes flashed her a warning as the woman appeared beside them again, two espresso cups in her hands.

'*Grazie,*' he said. He waited until she moved away again and then he shrugged his shoulders. 'Why not?' he asked Blair. 'It would be different, anyhow.'

'Let me get this straight,' Blair said. 'You're suggesting that I...no, it's too incredible! Not even you——' She broke off in mid-sentence.

'Come on, lady, don't stop now. Not even I...?'

She hesitated, and then she shrugged. What did she have to lose, after all? She was safe as long as he thought she was worth money to him, lots of money. And the little *trattoria* was too full of witnesses for him to do anything violent.

'You seized me against my will,' she said softly. 'Am I supposed to forget that?'

'I took you for damned good reasons,' he said sharply, hunching over the table and leaning towards her. 'Didn't you ever think of that?'

'I'll bet,' she said grimly. 'I...'

She closed her mouth as the woman placed a plate of little cakes in front of her.

'Queste sono bene, signorina,' she smiled.

Blair nodded. 'Thank you.' The woman hurried away and Blair leaned towards Hunter. 'People like you always have good reasons for what they do,' she whispered.

'And people like you should try and understand them.'

'My God,' she said, staring at him in disbelief, 'what are you, Hunter? An armchair psychiatrist? Do you really believe in the Stockholm Syndrome?'

'What?'

'The Stockholm Syndrome. Come on, you can't fool me. Someone who does what you do for a living must know all about it. That's the theory that says hostages, given time, begin to empathise with their captors.'

Hunter laughed harshly. 'It's not the theory I was questioning, Miss Desmond—it's the thought of you ever feeling sympathy for anyone but yourself.'

'*Me*, feel sympathy for *you*? You've got to be crazy!'

He sighed wearily and sipped at his coffee. 'Yeah, I guess maybe I am. Well, it's not as if I didn't know what

I was getting myself into. They told me what you were like. They...'

'They?'

Hunter smiled grimly. 'That's enough, Blair. You're not going to make me forget what I'm supposed to be doing. Come on, finish up. We've got a lot of driving ahead of us.'

She watched as he drank the rest of his coffee, and then she sighed. He wasn't about to say anything more. And what did it matter who 'they' were? His accomplices weren't here; she had only this man to deal with. And so far, at least, he hadn't really hurt her.

'Eat the cakes,' he said. 'We won't be stopping again for quite a while.'

She started to say no and then changed her mind. It would be silly to let herself grow weak. She'd need her strength when the chance for escape came. Blair picked up one of the cakes and bit into it. It was delicious, and it reminded her of just how hungry she really was. She finished it and ate the next, then licked the crumbs from her fingers. When finally she looked up, Hunter was grinning at her.

'I didn't think they taught you to do that in finishing school.'

'You're an awful snob, Mr Hunter!'

He laughed softly. 'Is that the worst thing you can call me, Blair? Hell, I guess I haven't been trying hard enough.' He shoved back his chair and rose. 'OK, time to move out.'

She stood as he began to burrow in his pocket for change. His face was averted, his back towards her. *Now,* she thought suddenly, and she sprinted for the door. In one quick movement, she yanked it open and raced towards the Lamborghini.

'Hey—dammit, Blair, what the hell...'

Hunter's voice rang out behind her but she ignored it. If she were lucky, the keys might still be in the car. And, even if they weren't, they were in a town, a place where someone would speak at least enough English to help her. Surely she could make someone understand what was happening to her?

She reached the car and pulled open the door. No keys, dammit! She glanced up; there was a young man across the narrow street, watching her.

'*Signor, per favore...*'

She gasped as strong hands clasped her shoulders and spun her around. Hunter's fingers dug into her flesh; in some distant part of her mind, she realised she'd have bruises on her skin the next day.

'That's a cute stunt,' he growled, pulling her towards him. 'Remind me never to turn my back on you again.'

Her eyes glared into his, and then she looked beyond his shoulder. The door to the *trattoria* hung open; a handful of its former occupants stood clustered in front of the building, watching the scene intently. Blair took a deep breath.

'Do any of you speak English?' she called.

'I'll kill you, Blair...'

Hunter's voice was a harsh whisper. His hands were biting into her now, and from the corner of her eye she saw the ugly expression on his face. But what was there to lose? One way or another, it would all end soon. He'd ask for ransom, and Oscar Desmond would refuse to pay it and it would all be over. Hunter would have a useless hostage on his hands. And he'd be frustrated and angry...

'Please, does anybody understand me?' she cried. 'This man—this man is...'

'Damn you to hell, Blair!'

He pulled her to him so roughly that she lost her balance and fell against the hard length of his body.

Hunter's hands left her shoulders and cupped her face. Her heart thudded.

'No, don't,' she begged, but it was too late.

His head bent to hers as his hands held her captive, and she whimpered as his mouth covered hers. His lips were hard and punishing. She tried to speak, to call out against his mouth, and immediately she felt the thrust of his tongue. Speech was impossible. Even getting a breath was out of the question. She tried to twist away from him, but he held her fast, his hands steadying her head, his body taking the full weight of hers. Tears filled her eyes. She wanted to hit him, to scratch him, to bite him—but all she could do was let him kiss her, not that this was a real kiss, she thought wildly. He was forcing her to submit to the touch of his mouth, forcing her to submit to the hard caress of his body. And yet...and yet...

Oh, God, it was happening again! There was a slow, hot fire spreading in her loins, licking its way along every nerve and muscle. No, thought Blair, no, please! But her lips were softening beneath his. And her legs were trembling. She was...she was melting, melting...

Hunter pushed her from him. Her eyes opened slowly, the thick lashes damp with tears.

'Jesus!' he said softly.

Her face lifted to his, and humiliation flooded through her as she looked at him. He was looking at her as if they were alone. The pewter flatness in his eyes had been replaced by a luminous silver flame. Blair shuddered as Hunter's glance travelled over her slowly, moving from her wide eyes to her slightly swollen mouth.

'Jesus,' he murmured again.

Blair swallowed. 'Why did you do that?' she whispered.

'I... I...' He ran his hand through his hair. 'Why the hell do you think?' he demanded roughly. 'Did you really think I'd let you get away with that crap? What you need is a gag.'

Colour sprang to her cheeks. Of course. What was the matter with her, anyway? She'd been calling for help. That was why he'd kissed her. To silence her. To stop her. She glanced over his shoulder. The group of men were whispering among themselves. She opened her mouth, and Hunter's arm slid around her waist.

'Hey, *signori*,' he yelled, *'e uno spettacolo splendido, si?'*

A string of musical Italian words poured from Hunter's lips. His tone was light, humourous, and after a couple of minutes the old men began to chuckle and then to laugh aloud. The younger man across the road sighed and nodded in apparent agreement.

'What did you tell them?' Blair muttered.

Hunter's arm tightened around her. 'That women are the same all over, that they need a little rough handling once in a while.'

'They won't buy that.'

His lips drew back from his teeth. 'They already have. This is the old world, Blair, not the playgrounds you're used to. Now be quiet, or I'll shut you up again. Get into the car.'

She climbed into the Lamborghini stiffly, buckling her seat-belt before he had the chance to order her to do it. Hunter got into the driver's seat and started the engine.

'Wave and smile to our admirers, Blair. Do it!' he rasped when she didn't comply.

She waved mechanically, falling back against the seat as the car roared away from the *trattoria*. She sat silently while the engine climbed from gear to gear, until she was sure the little restaurant was far behind them, and then she turned stiffly towards Hunter.

'Don't ever do that again,' she said softly. 'Do you hear me?'

He looked over at her and then back at the road. His hands tightened on the wheel.

'Don't make empty threats, Blair,' he said softly. 'You know damned well you liked it.'

She stared at him for what seemed an eternity, and then she lay her head back on the seat and turned her face to the window. God help me, she thought, closing her eyes, he's right!

CHAPTER FOUR

BLAIR'S eyes flew open and she stared into the darkness. For a fraction of a heartbeat she wondered where she was, and then, all too soon, she remembered. She was still an unwilling passenger in the Lamborghini, still trapped in this narrow space with her abductor. And they were still racing north into the night. Finding compass points wasn't her strong suit, but even she had finally figured out in which direction they were travelling.

She shifted carefully in the leather seat, trying to ease her aching muscles without calling Hunter's attention to the fact that she was awake. How long had she been asleep? she wondered. An hour? Two? The last thing she remembered was watching the sun turn the hills orange and gold. And Hunter's voice. It was the first time he'd spoken to her since they'd left the *ristorante*.

'Get some sleep,' he'd said roughly. 'We have a long way to go.'

Her response had been automatic. 'I'm not tired,' she'd said, but it hadn't been true. She'd been exhausted, as worn mentally as she was physically, and as the landscape grew dark, she'd finally put her head back and closed her eyes, falling quickly into deep, dreamless sleep.

Not that it had helped much. She was still tired. The headache she'd lied about earlier was a real one now, making her wince each time she moved her head. And she ached from hours of sitting in the cramped confines of the car. How much longer would this go on? she thought, and then she shuddered. The worst might still lay ahead. There was no way to know what lay at the end of this endless journey. Perhaps Hunter was planning to cross the border. Switzerland lay in this direction, and Austria, even Yugoslavia. Fear knotted her gut. How would anyone ever find her there?

Don't think about it, Blair. Think positively.

Positively. All right, then maybe he was taking her to some hideout in Italy. Maybe his accomplices were waiting for him. Maybe they wouldn't be quite as careful in their treatment of her as Hunter had been. Maybe, once he had her in some safe, out-of-the-way place, someone would be careless. Maybe...

'Are you awake?'

Blair swallowed. 'Yes,' she said, making her voice flat, trying not to betray her concern.

'You slept for a long time. How's the headache?'

She wondered, for a second, how he knew she had one, and then she remembered the lie she'd told him earlier.

'Not terrific,' she said. 'Are we stopping soon?'

She felt him turn towards her, and she kept her eyes riveted on the blackness ahead.

'Soon,' he said non-committally.

'How soon?'

'I'm afraid I can't give you an exact time,' he said, his words weighted with sarcasm. 'An hour, give or take a few minutes. Is that good enough?'

'No,' she said sharply, and she felt a rush of heat to her cheeks. 'I have to go to the bathroom,' she said, deliberately saying the words clearly and without hesitation. It was humiliating enough to have to announce her need, as if she were a child. She wasn't about to make things worse by dancing around the subject.

'Can't you wait?' he asked impatiently.

'Can't you miss a chance to embarrass me?' she snapped. 'No, I cannot wait. You'll have to find a place to stop. A hotel or a garage...' She spun towards him at the sound of his laughter. 'I'm glad you find this so amusing, Mr Hunter.'

He shook his head. 'Your arrogance amazes me, Miss Desmond. Where in hell do you think you're going to find a garage or a hotel? I'm sure the comfort facilities on the roads around Monte Carlo or Gstaad are luxurious, but there's not much call for such things in Tuscany.'

Tuscany. They they were somewhere near Florence, weren't they? Wasn't that what she'd seen on the map in the Alitalia magazine? 'People are people, Mr Hunter,' she said stiffly. 'And we all have the same needs.'

He sighed. 'All right, Blair, you've made your point. Just hang on a second...'

She grasped the dashboard as the car skidded to the side of the road. It slowed to a stop, the engine still running.

'Well, go on,' he said, reaching across her and opening the door. 'Make it fast.'

'Go on... You mean, you mean just...' She stared into the darkness and then at the man beside her. 'You mean you want me to... to...'

He grinned. '*I* don't want you to do anything. This was your idea, remember?'

'But there's nothing here. Just a field.' She stared at him, and then she turned away quickly and stepped from the car, cheeks burning. The night was as black as any she could recall. It was pointless to even try and escape, she thought, looking ahead. She was in a fenced field as far as she could tell, although she couldn't see further than a foot or so in any direction. Tall grass brushed against her trousered legs as she slipped through a gate. Something skittered underfoot and she faltered, stifling the desire to cry out, knowing it would only make Hunter laugh, and she'd given him more than enough chance to do that in the past few moments. There was a lone tree a few paces ahead, a cypress by its shadowy outline, and she marched towards it, hoping it would provide adequate shelter. A few moments later, she stalked back to the car. Head held high, she opened the door and climbed in.

'Feeling better?'

'I'm amazed you trusted me to go off on my own,' she said, staring straight ahead and deliberately ignoring his remark.

He gave a snort of laughter. 'Trust didn't have a damned thing to do with it.' He took a tubular, black object from the back seat. 'This is a starlight scope,' he said. 'You couldn't have hidden from me, even in the dark.' He glanced at her, and then back at the road. 'I'll always be one step ahead of you, Blair,' he said softly. 'Just keep that in mind before you try anything foolish.'

'My head hurts,' she said sharply. 'I need some aspirin.'

Hunter sighed again. 'Try the glove compartment. There should be a tin of aspirin in it.'

She leaned forwards and opened the compartment. To her surprise, it was messy, not neat and well organised as she'd expected. She rummaged through it, finding old road maps, half a pack of mints, some loose coins. And then, finally, her fingers closed around a small tin. She pulled it towards her, and as she did something clattered into her lap. Cassette recordings, she realised, and then Hunter's hand brushed against her arm.

'We might as well have music,' he said, taking the tapes from her lap. 'Any particular preferences?'

'Yes,' she said drily. 'An old vaudeville song—it's called "Show Me the Way to Go Home". Do you know it?'

Hunter laughed as he pushed the button on the cassette player. 'Relax, Blair. We'll be there soon.'

Where? she wondered, popping two aspirin tablets into her mouth. Not home. Not anywhere even approximating home. She made a face and forced the tablets down her dry throat. And then what? The thought of meeting with Hunter's accomplices terrified her, yet the thought of spending the night alone with him terrified her even more. He hadn't referred to what had happened at the *trattoria*. And he hadn't tried to touch her since. Not that that meant a damned thing. He'd taken advantage of her twice already, hadn't he? And he'd made it clear he'd do it again, if it suited his purposes. The thing to do, then, was not to give him the opportunity. She'd do as she was told and . . .

The rich sounds of a symphony orchestra filled the car, and Blair turned towards Hunter, her eyebrows arched in stunned surprise.

'The Albinoni Adagio?' She could no more have kept herself from speaking than she could have sprouted wings and flown. 'Is that your tape? I mean, does it belong to you?'

There was a second's pause before Hunter replied. 'Yes,' he said coldly. 'Doesn't it meet with your approval?'

'I didn't mean that. I . . . I love Albinoni. I just didn't, I mean, nobody . . .'

'You expected something else, is that correct? Torquemada and the Grand Inquisitors, perhaps, or the Four Horsemen and the Apocalypse . . .'

'No,' Blair said again, 'I just never . . .'

'Never pictured someone like me enjoying it, is that right?'

Dear God, she thought, I've antagonised him. 'I never thought about what you might enjoy one way or the other,' she said calmly. 'It's just that you don't often stumble across anyone who likes baroque music.'

She heard him let out his breath. 'And I'd never have guessed you'd recognise a symphony, much less something by Albinoni,' he said after a bit. 'So I guess that makes us even.'

She nodded stiffly. She'd have to watch herself, she thought. There was no point in angering him. Her safety—her very life—might depend on it. The poignant strains of the music flowed over her. He'd been right, of course, she thought, stealing a surreptitious glance at him. She had, indeed, been stunned at his taste in music. What was that saying? 'Music has charms to soothe a savage breast...'

Blair's eyes closed and her lips curved upwards. Torquemada and the Grand Inquisitors, for heaven's sake! Here she sat, racing through the night in a car with a man who liked classical music, a man with a quick intelligence and a sense of humour, a man whose kisses made her tremble...

A man who abducted you for ransom, Blair! Have you forgotten that?

Her eyes flew open and she sat up straight in the seat. What in God's name was happening to her? Was she crazy? Hunter was her enemy! He was her captor. He had kidnapped her, and now he was taking her to some unknown place where anything might happen, anything...

Hunter's gruff voice broke into her thoughts. 'We're here. End of the line, Blair. Let's go.'

Her heart began to thud like a caged bird beating its wings in fear. They were parked on a hilltop; she could see the hulking shape of a small house beside the car. Hunter came around to her side and opened the door.

'Watch your step,' he said. 'The ground is uneven.'

She got out of the car stiffly, ignoring his outstretched hand. End of the line, he'd said. Was that just a poor choice of words, or was it something more?

'Hunter,' she said with sudden urgency, 'listen, I...'

'Come on,' he said impatiently. 'Get moving.'

She took a hesitant step forwards, and then another. It was too dark to see anything, but she sensed that they were in some isolated place, far from any town. Gravel crunched softly underfoot; she smelled the faint scent of jasmine on the night breeze. Hunter's hand closed around her wrist.

'There are three steps here. Easy on the second one— it sags a little.'

She tried to draw away from him, but that only made his fingers close around her more tightly. I won't run, she wanted to tell him, not now, not when my legs can barely support me, but she seemed to be having trouble breathing. He was speaking to her again, but she couldn't hear him over the heavy beat of her heart. His hand slipped to her waist, lying heavy against her thin cotton sweater.

'Wait,' he was saying, and finally she nodded.

She heard the jingle of keys and the door swung open. *The end of the line,* she thought again, staring into impenetrable blackness. Hunter's hand urged her forwards.

'Let's go,' he murmured.

Blair swallowed. 'I can't see anything, Hunter.'

'You don't have to see anything. Just move.'

'Just tell me if...'

'Move, dammit!'

His hand slid to the small of her back and propelled her forwards. The heavy darkness of the house closed around her as the door swung shut. She stood absolutely still, all her senses sharp, expectant, trying to acclimatise herself to her surroundings.

'Could... could you turn on a light? Please?' She heard the fear in her voice and hated herself for it. Could Hunter hear it, too?

'In a minute,' he said. The sound of his footsteps echoed across the floor. 'Just let me...OK, I've got it.'

She heard the scrape of a match, saw its yellow flare in the dark, and then an eerie golden glow lit the room, throwing Hunter's face into terrifying relief. He held a kerosene lantern in his hand, and she watched as he adjusted the flame to a warm, yellow glow. Then he set the lantern on a table and walked towards her.

'Are we... isn't there anyone else here?'

He smiled unpleasantly. 'No, there's no staff, Blair. Sorry.'

'Isn't there... isn't there any electricity?'

'No electricity, no indoor plumbing, no room service. I knew you'd love it here.'

Blair glanced cautiously around the room. It looked worn and old. A farmhouse, she thought, looking at the roughly hewn table on which Hunter had placed the lantern. A woodstove and some cupboards lined one wall. There was a sink next to the stove; water dripped slowly from a pump-handled spigot into the rusted basin.

Hunter was watching her with a strange expression on his face. 'What's the matter, Blair?' he asked softly. 'Are you frightened?'

'Why should I be frightened?' she asked quickly, hoping she sounded more positive than she felt. She took a steadying breath. 'It's in your best interests to keep me safe, isn't it, Mr Hunter?'

He nodded. 'That's the name of the game, yes.'

It wasn't the end of the line, then. Blair turned away from him, almost shuddering with relief.

'I see we have running water,' she said into the silence.

'Such as it is. It's fresh and clean, but cold as hell.' Hunter jerked his head to the rear. 'There's an outhouse out back.'

'Well, then,' she said brightly, 'we have all the amenities. A kitchen, a bathroom, water...'

'And a bed.'

He had spoken softly, almost in a whisper. Blair looked across the room at him. He was staring at her with narrowed eyes, a faint half-smile on his mouth. Her heartbeat quickened.

'The Tuscany Hilton,' she said in that same brightly artificial voice, carefully ignoring what he'd said and the way in which he'd said it. 'You did say we were in Tuscany, didn't you?'

'Does it matter?'

Blair walked across the room. 'Of course it matters. How can I send postcards to all my friends if I don't know where we are?' Her voice trembled and broke on the last few words. *Don't fall apart now, Blair*...

'What is it, Blair? Is the headache worse?'

She shook her head. She could feel the sudden pressure of tears in her eyes and she bit down on her lower lip. 'No,' she said sharply. 'I ... I just ...' Her voice broke again and she turned away so he couldn't see her face. 'I just... I'm upset, that's all. I don't suppose you could possibly understand that, Mr Hunter. Not that it would matter to you. Not that ...'

To her horror, her voice gave way and tears trickled down her cheeks.

'Blair...' Hunter cursed softly. She heard his footsteps moving towards her, and then his arms went around her and she felt the hardness of his chest against her back. 'Easy,' he murmured, 'easy. I know this is rough...'

'Let go of me,' she sobbed, but when he drew her back against him she sighed.

'You're tired,' he said quietly. 'You'll feel better in the morning.'

She could hear the steady beat of his heart beneath her ear. Her eyes closed slowly as she let the warmth of his body begin to chase the chill from hers.

'Things won't be any different in the morning,' she said wearily.

He turned her slowly in his arms and looked down at her. 'They will,' he murmured. 'Trust me.'

Blair looked up at him through her damp lashes. 'Trust you?' she whispered. 'Why should I?'

Hunter's hand moved slowly down her back, and she drew in her breath at his touch.

'Blair,' he said thickly, 'Blair...'

Her hands came up to push him away, but somehow her palms lay limp against his chest instead. His head was bending towards her; his arms were tightening around her, her lashes were drooping over her eyes...

'I don't want to make this rougher for you than it has to be,' he whispered, his breath warm against her cheek. 'Just promise me you'll behave, Blair, and...'

Her arms circled around his back, sliding down his torso to his waist as he drew her closer. He felt so good, so... Suddenly, her eyes flew open. He had... God, he had a gun tucked into his trousers, lying snugly in the small of his back. How had she missed it earlier? What was she doing? Was she crazy? Anger flooded through her, at herself as much as at him. She pushed him from her with all the strength she could muster.

'You're right,' she snapped, 'I am tired. Otherwise I wouldn't have listened to you for even a second. What kind of fool do you take me for, Hunter? I know what your game is—we're back to the Stockholm Syndrome again, aren't we? Did you just realise you bit off more than you can chew? Well, if you're counting on me to help guard myself, you can forget about it!' His arms fell to his sides and his expression hardened, but it was too late. She wasn't finished yet, and she was damned if she was going to stop now! 'I'm telling you right now,

Hunter, I'll get out of this...this hovel, and away from you the very first chance I get. The very first. The...'

Suddenly, her bravado faded and reality crashed down around her. Hunter smiled grimly, his eyes as cold as ice.

'Thank you for warning me, Blair,' he said in that silky-smooth voice she knew all too well. 'You've made my job much easier. Now that I know your intentions, I simply won't give you the opportunity.' His hand closed around her wrist.

'Wait... Hunter, wait! I...I didn't mean all that. I told you that you were right, didn't I? I'm just tired, I... What are you doing? Where are we going? Hunter, please, answer me...'

'We're going to the outhouse,' he said, snatching up the lantern as he dragged her after him. 'And then we're going to bed.'

'I...I don't have to go to the outhouse. And you can forget all those things I said. I... Dammit, Hunter, don't you hear me? I said...' Her voice trembled as he kicked open a door at the rear of the kitchen and tugged her through to the room beyond. In the wavering glow of the lantern, she saw a four-poster bed that seemed to take up most of the room.

'No outhouse? OK, Blair, then you can wait here for me.' He put his hand in the small of her back and pushed; she fell face-down in a sprawl across the bed. He was on her before she could move, his legs straddling her body, his hand grasping her wrists, pulling them behind her. She heard the whisper of leather on fabric, and then something snaked around her wrists—his belt, she re-alised as she felt its cool touch against her skin.

'Hunter, don't,' she sobbed, but it was too late. The bed squeaked as he got to his feet, she heard a door slam, and he was gone.

She buried her face in the blanket and let the tears she'd so long suppressed roll down her cheeks. She'd been so careful all day, so cautious, only making a rash move that one time she'd tried to run, all the time weighing her words, planning her actions, doing everything she could to protect herself from him, and now she'd ruined everything. How could she have been so stupid? Anger, self-pity, whatever it was, she'd let it get the best of her, and look what had happened. Here she was, trussed up like a Christmas turkey, at the mercy of a dangerous criminal...

The door slammed again. *Oh, God*...

'Hunter, listen, I'll be good, I promise. I...'

'Don't beg,' he said grimly. 'It doesn't become you.'

Blair nodded. 'If you'd just listen to me for a minute,' she said quickly. 'I know I've insulted you...'

'Insulted me?' His laughter was harsh and brief. 'You haven't insulted me, Miss Desmond, you've simply confirmed my opinion of you.'

Blair heard the whisper of fabric. 'What... what are you doing, Hunter?' she asked.

From the corner of her eye, she saw his black sweater hit the floor. 'I'm getting ready for bed, Miss Desmond,' he said tonelessly. 'What the hell do you think I'm doing?'

'But... I... I'm hungry,' she said desperately. 'Aren't we going to have some dinner?'

He laughed again. She saw him put the gun on the table beside the bed. 'Sorry, Miss Desmond, the kitchen at the Tuscany Hilton closed an hour ago. You'll just have to wait until morning.'

She swallowed drily, wondering if she could get enough saliva into her mouth so she could speak.

'H... Hunter, look, what happened before—what I said—can't you forget it? Can't we go back to the way things were?'

She recoiled as his shoes clattered against the stone floor. 'That's exactly what we're doing, Miss Desmond,' he said. Blair closed her eyes as she heard the metallic slither of a zipper. 'We're going back to the way things should be. I almost let myself think you were human for a while. But you reminded me that you aren't. You're Meryl Blair Desmond. I know all about you.' She gasped as he clutched her shoulders and pulled her to a sitting position. 'You'd rather die than spend a night in a— what did you say, Miss Desmond? You'd rather die than spend a night in this hovel with a man like me.'

'Hunter, I didn't mean it...'

Tears were streaming freely down her cheeks as he freed her wrists. 'Of course you meant it,' he snarled. 'Actually, I'm grateful to you for reminding me of our relationship.'

Blair rubbed her hands across her eyes. 'I...I didn't mean it the way it sounded, Hunter. Really...' She looked up at him and the plea died in her throat. In the warm glow of the lantern, the planes of his chest gleamed golden against the shadows of the room. Dark hair lay whorled across his skin, tapering to a line that vanished finally beneath his trousers. He'd opened just the top of the zipper, and the trousers hung low on his hips. She looked back to his face, trying to think of something to say that would diffuse the sudden tension in the room, but her mind was blank.

'It's bed time, Blair,' he said softly, a cold smile twisting his hard mouth.

'I'm...I'm not tired,' she said quickly.

He smiled again. 'But I am.'

'Hunter, listen, I...'

'Get your clothes off.'

Blair shook her head. 'No,' she said softly.

'We've gone through this before,' he said. 'We can do this the easy way or the hard way.'

'I thought you said you had to keep me safe...'

He smiled grimly. 'You're safe when I say you are, Blair.'

She ran her tongue across her dry lips. 'Don't do this, Hunter,' she whispered. 'I beg you...'

'I told you, don't beg,' he said, lifting her to her feet. 'Come on, Blair, get undressed.'

'You don't really want to do this,' she said desperately. 'You...Hunter,' she gasped, 'don't...'

She struck out at him as he began to slide her sweater up her midriff, but he ignored her.

'It's been one hell of a long day, Blair,' he said. 'I've driven over half of Italy, I've put up with your nastiness and your whining, and I'm tired.' She gasped as he tugged the sweater over her head and tossed it aside.

'I'll scream,' she said.

'There's no one but me to hear you,' he said softly. 'And once I grow weary of listening...' His eyes flashed a cold warning. 'Don't push me, Blair,' he said softly. 'I may have indulged you this morning, but that was God knows how many hours and how many miles ago, and my patience is beginning to wear thin. Now, will you finish the job, or shall I?'

Tears coursed silently down her cheeks as she numbly eased the white trousers down her legs.

'Get them off,' he growled. 'The shoes, too.'

She kicked off her canvas flats and then the trousers, her eyes on his face all the while, until finally she stood before him wearing only a skimpy cotton camisole that barely fell below her breasts and a pair of matching bikini panties. A breeze from the open window drifted across her skin and she shivered, even though the night air was warm.

'Hunter,' she said, the single word a plea.

His eyes met hers and she saw that curious flatness in them again, and then his gaze moved over her slowly, dispassionately, as if she were a plaster mannequin. She waited for him to speak, but he said nothing. The silence between them grew and still she waited, barely breathing.

'Hunter,' she said again, 'please...'

Her pulse began to race erratically. His eyes met hers again, but it was different this time. The flatness was gone, replaced by that bright silver flame that seemed to sear her flesh. She felt a wave of heat lick at her body as he took a step forwards.

'No,' she whispered, 'please...'

Her voice was thin. It was a stranger's voice, one she'd never heard before. Blair suddenly felt as if time had stopped. A trickle of cold sweat crept down between her breasts. She heard the laboured rasp of her breath, or was it Hunter's? The shallow rise and fall of his chest was as rapid as her own. The air in the bedroom was suddenly heavy with jasmine from the night wind. Hunter muttered something and took another step towards her. Her nostrils filled with the clean, heated scent of him.

'Hunter?'

Her whisper was as insubstantial as the petals of a fallen flower, but it stopped him. He stared at her, frozen, while an eternity ticked by in a second, and then he slammed his fist into his hand.

'Get on the bed,' he said in a rough whisper. 'Go on, dammit! Now!'

Blair sank to the mattress. The strength to fight him was gone. She had done all she could; what came next was beyond her control. He took her hand and she felt the light touch of the belt as he looped it around her wrist. She closed her eyes tightly, just as if she were a little girl back in Iowa. It was what she'd always done to block out something terrible, something dreadful, like visits to the dentist or the doctor or...

'Goodnight, Blair,' Hunter said gruffly.

Her eyes flew open as she felt the weight of him settle on the mattress beside her. He had tied the other end of the belt around his own wrist; as she watched, he lay the gun on the bed, piled her clothing on it, tucked the makeshift pillow beneath his head and closed his eyes.

'Goodnight?' Her voice was a whisper.

Hunter yawned. 'Even if you could loosen the belt without waking me, which I doubt—even if you could manage it, you won't get far without your clothes.' He turned his head towards her. His eyes, she saw, had become a clouded grey. 'Your underwear is probably a big success on the pages of Vogue, but I don't think it would take you very far in these hills. Pleasant dreams.'

He reached out and turned down the flame of the lantern, then stretched lightly, like a cat. She stared at him in stunned disbelief as his eyes closed. In the lantern's half-light, his sooty lashes lay thickly against his cheeks. After what could have been no more than a minute, she could tell by the even rise and fall of his chest that he was asleep.

Blair turned her face to the ceiling. Of course he'd fall asleep easily. What was there to keep him awake? He hadn't suffered the kind of terrifying day she had. He hadn't just been scared half out of his mind. He would sleep—snore, probably—while she lay awake the whole night . . . while she . . . while she . . .

Her lashes fluttered to her cheeks and she slept. Some time during the night, the wind changed. A sudden damp chill blew through the window and into the room, but neither of the people on the bed noticed it. In their sleep, they had turned towards each other. Curled in Hunter's arms, Blair slept a dreamless sleep.

CHAPTER FIVE

SUNLIGHT was streaming into the bedroom when Blair awoke. She was alone, although the warm imprint of Hunter's body still creased the sheet beside her. Her fingers went immediately to her wrist, rubbing the chafed skin, tracing the faint line his belt had left. Damn the man!

There was a light blanket over her, although she couldn't remember using it the night before. Clutching it to her chin, she sat up and pushed the hair out of her eyes. The door was ajar, and she could hear noises from the other room, which meant that he was out there. Not that she'd expected him to be anywhere else. A man who stripped you of your clothes and tied you up to make sure you didn't get away wasn't very likely to wander off while you were asleep!

Her clothing was still piled on the mattress beside her, where he'd left it. If she hurried, she could get dressed while she was still alone, without his cool grey eyes watching her. Her white trousers were creased from having served as his pillow. She pulled them on quickly swinging her legs to the floor and closing the zipper with trembling fingers. Hunter wasn't going to get her clothes away from her again, not without one hell of a fight. He'd said he took them from her to keep her from trying to escape, but she knew there was more to it than that. There was a psychological disadvantage in being almost naked. Last night, when he'd looked at her, she'd felt vulnerable. And something more, something...

Stop it! She eased the sweater over her head, pulling it down past her uncombed hair. The sweater was still warm with the heat of Hunter's body. And it smelled of him, she realised suddenly. She closed her eyes and inhaled deeply, wondering if he ever used cologne or after-shave, hoping he didn't, hoping he always smelled just this way...

'Are you crazy?' she whispered aloud. 'You must be. You...'

'It's caffeine withdrawal,' Hunter said from the doorway, his voice low and sleep-roughened. Blair looked up in surprise and he grinned at her. His dark hair was tousled, his chest was bare. He was wearing denim jeans, slung low on his hips. 'Good morning,' he said pleasantly. 'Did you have a good night?'

Colour rose to her cheeks. 'Good morning,' she said stiffly. 'Where did you say the outhouse was?'

He nodded towards the main room. 'Through there and to the back. There's a door in the rear. You can't miss it.'

'Thank you,' she said formally. 'I don't suppose you've seen my shoes?'

He grinned again. 'As a matter of fact, I have.'

'Well? Where are they, then?' she asked impatiently. 'I need them if I'm going outside.'

Hunter shrugged his shoulders. 'The outhouse is only a few paces from the house. Even your tender feet can manage that.'

'Will you just tell me where my shoes are, Hunter? I...'

'No shoes,' he said, shaking his head. 'You only get them when I can keep an eye on you.'

'For God's sake,' she said angrily, 'this is insane! First my clothing, and now my shoes?'

He shrugged again. 'Why not think of it this way, Blair? You've improved your lot from last night. Bare feet are better than bare...'

'You're insufferable!' she snapped, stalking past him.

He laughed. 'Coffee will be ready when you get back,' he said. 'Maybe that'll improve your disposition.'

The rich, strong aroma of brewing coffee embraced her as she entered the kitchen moments later. Hunter was still half-dressed, she noticed, her eyes sliding away from him as he padded from an open cupboard to the table. But he'd combed his hair and splashed water on his face—she could see drops of it glistening on his skin.

'Your carry-on's in the bedroom,' he said. 'I thought you might want your toothbrush or something.'

Blair nodded stiffly and walked past him. The stone floor, polished to smoothness by generations of use, was warm beneath her bare feet. She ran a comb through her tangled hair, remembering how Hunter had re-arranged it yesterday. It seemed ironic that he'd unknowingly put it back to the way she'd worn it before Meryl had talked her into having it restyled. Her hair probably needed more than a combing, but she was in no mood to poke through the carry-on for her brush. What did it matter how she looked? Hunter was the only person who was going to see her.

She took her toothbrush into the kitchen and brushed her teeth at the rust-stained sink. The water was cold as ice, and she gasped as she splashed handfuls of it on her face. But she felt better when she'd finished, and, when Hunter handed her a chipped, earthenware mug filled with black coffee, she almost smiled at him. There was an open tin of tuna fish on the table, along with a package of water biscuits.

'Breakfast,' he said ruefully, perching on the edge of the table. 'I hope you don't take cream and sugar, because we haven't either.'

Blair sat down in a chair opposite him and lifted the cup to her lips. The coffee was rich and delicious. Her eyes closed with pleasure as it slipped down her throat.

'Good?' he asked.

Her eyes opened and she stared at him. 'Good,' she admitted finally. 'Very good, as a matter of fact.'

He grinned. 'Half the tuna's yours,' he said, pushing the tin towards her. 'More, if you like. I remember you said you were hungry last night. In fact, you seemed more interested in food than in going to bed.'

His eyes glinted with amusement. Blair felt a flush rise up from her breasts towards her face.

'We didn't go to bed, Hunter.'

'Didn't we?'' he asked with great innocence. 'Funny, I could have sworn we did. How else could I have awakened with your head cradled on my shoulder this morning, Blair?'

'My head was not on your shoulder,' she said quickly.

'We were sleeping together...'

'We were *not* sleeping together. We simply went to bed...'

'Which was what I said in the first place.'

His voice had a smug, self-assured tone. Blair started to answer and then thought better of it. Instead, she shoved the tin of tuna towards him and pushed her chair back from the table.

Hunter's eyebrows rose. 'Don't tell me you're not going to tuck into this feast I prepared for you.'

'Enjoy it yourself,' she said stiffly. 'I'm not much for tuna.'

'I'm sure you're not,' he said carefully. 'Matter of fact, I'd prefer bacon and eggs, or croissants, or damned near anything else myself. But tuna's the only item on the menu this morning.'

'Then I'll just have coffee, thank you.'

'Eat up, Blair,' he said softly. 'I don't want you to starve to death on my account.'

'No,' she said, her eyes cold, 'I'm sure you wouldn't. I wouldn't be worth anything to you then, would I?'

'That's true,' he said, 'but that's not what I was thinking.'

His eyes roved over her, mentally stripping away her trousers and sweater, and she knew he was thinking of how she'd looked the night before. All at once, nothing mattered more than keeping herself fit and strong, and surviving the ordeal she was suffering at his hands.

'I don't really give a damn about what you were thinking, Hunter,' she said, pulling the tin of tuna towards her. 'But you're right. There's no sense in going hungry.' She forked some tuna on a biscuit and bit into it. Not even caviar could have tasted better, she thought as she swallowed. She gulped the remaining biscuit down and licked the crumbs from her fingers.

Hunter laughed softly. 'Good?'

It was useless to try and pretend otherwise. Blair sighed and nodded her head. 'Wonderful,' she said through a mouthful of tuna. 'I can't remember the last time I was this...' She broke off and stared at him. 'Aren't you eating?'

'Later,' he said, waving his hand.

'But you haven't eaten since... You didn't even have any of those cakes yesterday. You...' She put down the biscuit as the tuna turned to paste in her mouth.

'Now what's wrong?' Hunter stared at her and began to laugh. 'God almighty, but you are the most suspicious woman,' he said, reaching for the remaining piece of her biscuit and popping it into his mouth. 'I admit, I'll do what has to be done to keep you here, Blair, but I'm not going to drug you.'

'You're only going to use restraints? Well, what a relief that is, Hunter. Remind me to thank you some time.'

'Now, now. There's no point in being sarcastic. Besides, the belt wasn't a restraint.' He lifted his coffee-cup to his lips and took a sip of the dark liquid.

'Wasn't it.' The words were a statement, not a question, and he shrugged.

'It was just an improvised security device, Blair.'

'You tied me up, Hunter. You . . .'

'I tied us together. There's a difference.'

'Not that I can see.'

'Really? Then I'll tie you to the bed tonight, instead of to my wrist,' he said bluntly. His eyes met hers and he sighed. 'Look, Blair, the sooner you settle down, the easier this will be for the both of us.'

'Settle down?'

'Yes, exactly. I know this isn't any fun for you, but . . .'

Blair snorted in disbelief. 'You certainly have a way with a phrase, Hunter. No, this isn't "fun"! Being frightened never is—not for most people, anyway. Maybe for someone like you . . .'

'There's nothing to be frightened of,' he said softly.

Her laughter was harsh and swift. 'Isn't there?'

Hunter shook his head. 'No, not now. Getting here safely was the difficult part, but we seem to have managed that all right.'

'You mean—we're going to stay here?'

He nodded. 'Yes. I'm sure no one's followed us. And anyone who tries to get to us now will have a rough time of it.'

'What do you mean?' Panic sounded in the rush of words. 'You said we were still in Italy—in Tuscany . . .'

'Yes,' he said, adding coffee to his cup, 'that's right. We're in the hills north of Florence. But we're in a remote location, the kind of place nobody stumbles across. And we're on the top of a hill, far from a main road, with one hell of a clear view of the valley below . . .'

Blair trembled with a sudden chill. If she'd had any faint spark of hope left, Hunter's self-confident speech had just snuffed it out.

'What you're saying is that there's no chance they'll find us,' she said finally. 'Is that it?'

Hunter nodded. 'I can promise you that, Blair.'

She let out her breath in a long sigh. She thought of how easily, how professionally, he'd taken her twenty-four hours ago, how cleanly he'd evaded whatever pursuit the Desmonds and the Italian police must have mounted, and she knew it was useless to doubt his word. Whatever else he was, she was certain he was not a man who made idle promises.

'I see,' she said softly, setting down her coffee mug. 'Then—then, that's it.'

'For the time being, yes.'

'And... and we're alone?'

He looked into her eyes and a half-smile curved across his lips. 'And we're alone. You asked me that last night, too. Don't you remember?'

'Did I?'

The smile flickered across his face again. 'What's the matter, Blair? Is the thought of a few days in my company unbearable?'

Her chin rose. 'And our sleeping arrangements?'

'What about them?'

'What do you mean, what about them? We can't...we can't keep sharing the bed.'

Hunter's gaze was even. 'Come on, Blair. You're not going to tell me you've never shared your bed with a man before, are you?'

'That's none of your business, Mr Hunter,' she said coolly.

His smile faded and he got to his feet. 'You're right,' he said coldly, 'it's not. *You're* my business, pure and simple.'

'Business,' she repeated softly, watching him as he cleared the table. 'Is that what you call the way you earn your living?'

'What do you call the way your father earns his?' he demanded, tossing the empty tins into a paper sack.

'Are you trying to make some kind of comparison between yourself and my...and an honest business-man? For God's sake, Hunter...'

'For God's sake, Blair,' he mimicked angrily, 'let's not make it sound as if your father is a philanthropist, OK? I do what I do, and Oscar Desmond does what he does, and that's it.' He glared at her angrily as he stuffed the loose biscuits back into the container. 'Just do me a favour and don't sound so noble.'

'I wasn't trying to sound anything, Mr Hunter. I was just...' Blair broke off in mid-sentence. The things he'd just said about Oscar Desmond's business empire kept tumbling through her mind. 'Are you saying—do you mean that all this has something to do with the labour problems at the Desmond mills?'

Hunter shrugged his shoulders. 'Maybe.'

'Maybe? Don't you know?'

'How would I? I just follow orders.' His voice faded as he walked into the bedroom. He came out again, slipping his shirt over his head. 'Yeah, maybe that's what triggered this kidnapping. It makes as much sense as anything, I guess.'

Blair shook her head. 'What kind of man are you, Hunter? Don't you need to know the reasons before—don't you believe in anything?'

Hunter spun towards her. She gasped as his hands shot out and grasped her shoulders. 'Who the hell do you think you are?' he snarled, hauling her to her feet.

'I wasn't trying to... I didn't mean to...' Blair's voice was breathless.

'I believe in my name, my word, and my honour.'

'I wasn't questioning your honour. I...'

'What the hell do you know about honour? Women like you...'

'Mr Hunter, I'm sorry. I swear, I...'

'And now it's *Mr* Hunter again. How touching!'

'You said to call you... it was your idea... I...'

Her voice trembled and broke. Hunter's eyes, dark with menace, burned into hers and then, suddenly, his hands fell from her shoulders and he took a deep breath.

'I'm sorry,' he said carefully. 'I didn't mean to frighten you. It was uncalled for.'

Dear God, she thought crazily, etiquette for every occasion! 'No, that's OK,' she said with equal care. 'It was... it was my fault, actually. I... I had no right to question your motives.'

'My motives are simple, Miss Desmond,' he said flatly. 'Money's one. Skill's another.'

'Skill? I don't understand.'

His smile was bitter and fleeting. 'This is all I know,' he said. 'It's what I've always done. It's what I'm best at.'

'But—surely there's something else?'

His eyes darkened and narrowed with memory. 'Once, maybe. At least, I thought there might be, but...' She held her breath as he reached towards her. His hand stroked her uncombed curls back from her face and then he turned away. 'We've got a lot to do, Blair.' His voice was suddenly impersonal as he flung open the cupboards. 'The tuna and biscuits were all I could find. So, if you don't want to go hungry, we'd best replenish our supplies.'

'I don't understand.'

'We're going to market,' he said cheerfully. 'Doesn't that sound like fun?'

She could feel the blood pounding in her veins, and it took all her effort to keep her voice from showing the sudden surge of hope she felt.

'To... You mean we're going into Florence?'

'Well, to a little town near Florence. We'll get some tinned foods, some fruits and vegetables, cheese, bread—perhaps even some meat. How does that sound?'

'It sounds... it sounds fine.'

'And then we'll make the call.'

Her head sprang up. 'A telephone call?'

Hunter's eyes met hers. 'That's what I said, Blair.' His voice was soft, almost caressing. 'I think it's about time we got in touch with your father, don't you?'

He said nothing else until they were in the Lamborghini. 'I hope I can trust you to behave yourself, Blair,' he said quietly. 'I'd hate to have to do anything unpleasant.'

'Does it make you feel good to threaten me, Hunter?' she demanded bitterly.

A muscle twitched in his jaw as he stared at her, and then he turned away and switched on the ignition.

'We're a man and a woman on holiday,' he said, putting on a pair of dark aviator glasses. 'Remember that, and we won't have any problems.'

She sat back stiffly as he pulled the car on to the rutted dirt track that led from the farmhouse. There was no choice but to do as he said, she thought, staring out at the softly rolling hills. He was quick and strong and, added to all that, he was armed. He'd given her her shoes after breakfast, and while she was putting them on she looked up and found him wiping a rag along a dull, black object which, she realised with a sudden start, was his gun. Her eyes had fixed on it.

'Are you...' Her voice was thin, and she swallowed and began again. 'Are you expecting trouble?'

He closed one eye and sighted along the barrel. 'I always expect trouble,' he said. He gave her a quick smile. 'There's nothing for you to worry about.'

'But you'd use that if you had to?' she asked in a papery whisper.

He nodded. 'If I had to,' he'd said, tucking the gun away at the small of his back. 'Let's hope that it doesn't come to that.'

He was what he was, she thought now, stealing a glance at him: a man who liked music, who hadn't done the things he could have when she was helpless during the long night, who'd insisted she eat her fill of their meagre rations—but he was a criminal. A killer, for all she knew. Just because he had civilised tastes, just because he looked as if he'd be as much at home in Los Angeles as he was here in these isolated hills, didn't mean that . . . Just because the sweetness of his mouth and the feel of his hands made her tremble, didn't mean that . . .

'What are you thinking?' he asked.

Blair folded her hands in her lap and looked down at them. 'Nothing,' she said.

There was a tremor in her voice. Hunter glanced at her and then, to her amazement, he reached across the console and put his hand over hers.

'It'll be all right, Blair,' he said softly.

Her eyes sought his. 'Will it?' she asked in a whisper.

He nodded. 'Yes. Before you know it, you'll be back in Rome, safe and sound, and all this will have all the substance of a dream.' He looked towards her and their eyes met. 'That's what you want, isn't it?'

She said nothing. Inexplicably, her eyes filled with tears. Hunter cursed under his breath and jammed his foot down on the brake pedal. The brakes squealed and the Lamborghini came to a shuddering stop on the narrow track.

The silence of the surrounding meadow seemed to wash over the car when he shut off the ignition. Somewhere nearby, a bird trilled a few notes into the sultry blue sky.

'Come here, dammit,' he said fiercely, and then she was in his arms, clinging tightly to his neck as his mouth took hers in a kiss that was at once sweeter yet more sensual than any she'd ever experienced. She felt the corner of the console bite into her hip as he lifted her towards him, but nothing was as important as the feel of his shoulders beneath her hands, the taste of his lips as they parted hers, the warmth of his body as she pressed against it. She moaned softly as his hand cupped her breast, as he pressed his palm to the length of her thigh. He was blazing with heat; she felt it through the layers of clothing that separated them, felt herself ignite beneath the caresses of his hands and his mouth. She was spinning in a vortex of emotions, out of control, wanting Hunter, wanting her captor to become her lover, wanting...

The annoyed bleating of a goat, followed by the sharp barks of a dog, broke them apart.

'My God!' Blair whispered shakily, putting her hand to her mouth, touching the tender flesh that was already swelling with the passion of his kiss. 'Hunter...'

'Come back here,' he growled, reaching for her again, but she shook her head.

'No,' she gasped, pressing her hands against his chest, 'no, we can't...'

'We'll go somewhere more private,' he said, running his hand along her cheek. 'The farmhouse...'

She closed her eyes. 'No,' she said more strongly, leaning away from him. 'This is—it's wrong.'

'It's right,' he murmured, reaching towards her. 'You know it is.'

Blair shook her head. 'Don't,' she said sharply. 'Never touch me again, Hunter.' She took a deep breath. 'Do you understand? Never.'

Coldness turned his eyes to ice, his mouth to a narrow, uncompromising line in his dark face.

His whisper made the hair rise on the nape of her neck. 'I understand, all right.' Suddenly, he reached across the narrow space that separated them, his hand curling around the back of her neck. She winced at the harsh pressure of his fingers. 'Never play with me, Blair,' he said, his voice a warning rasp in the quiet confines of the car, 'never. You'll get hurt.'

He pulled away from her and turned the key, jamming his foot to the floor as the engine growled to life. Blair fell back against the seat as the car gathered momentum. She risked a quick glance at Hunter and then wished she hadn't. His profile might have been carved of granite. There was an aggressive thrust to his head and shoulders; even the spread of his fingers on the gearstick seemed dangerous.

He *was* dangerous, she thought, staring blindly ahead as they sped through the golden morning. He was like a jungle cat, a creature whose deceptive beauty cloaked its deadly intent. And she was his prey. And yet... and yet, only a heartbeat ago, drowning in the flood of sweet fire he'd undammed within her, she'd gladly have died in his arms.

Blair shuddered, despite the heat of the August sun. Was this how the tiger's victim felt in the last moment? Was there some dark, blinding passion that linked predator and prey? Dear God, she wondered, what was happening to her?

CHAPTER SIX

THE Lamborghini bounced and skidded down the mountain path with almost reckless speed, slowing only when it reached an intersection with a hard-packed ribbon of dirt that stretched dustily between green fields. Hunter glanced into the mirror and then pushed the accelerator hard. The car roared in response and charged up the road, leaving plumes of red dust swirling in the air behind it. After they'd sped around a blind curve, Blair cleared her throat.

'Aren't you going awfully fast?'

Hunter's lips drew back from his teeth in something that was not quite a smile. 'Yes.'

Yes. Not 'maybe', not 'perhaps', not even 'am I?', Blair thought, stealing a glance at him. Just that one arrogant word tossed down like a gauntlet. Well, it was better than the silence in which they'd spent the last half-hour.

Hunter had been in a silent rage ever since he'd kissed her. No, she thought, not since he'd kissed her. Get it right, Blair. He kissed you and you melted in his arms, you let him think anything was possible, and then you told him never to touch you again...

'Never play with me,' he'd said, and she knew what that meant. He thought Meryl Desmond was toying with him. And, as bad as that was, it wasn't as bad as the truth, and God knew, she couldn't tell him that. She couldn't tell him she was Blair Nolan, not Meryl Desmond. Even if she could, there was no way to explain what she felt when he kissed her, when he looked into her eyes, when he whispered her name.

It was better not to try and analyse anything until she was safely out of this mess. Then she could try and make some sense out of it. Had other captives felt what she was feeling?

He's had you for two days, Blair. Not even that. Not even thirty-six hours...

'Get out your dark glasses and put them on.'

She blinked and turned towards him. 'I... what did you say?'

He looked at her and then back at the road. 'Put on your sunglasses,' he said. 'And keep them on until I tell you you can take them off.'

Blair dug into her purse and pulled out her glasses. Meryl's glasses, she thought, slipping the oversized frames on her nose.

'The town we're going to... what did you say it was called?'

'I didn't.'

'Hunter, look, I... I'm sorry for what happened.'

'You don't owe me any apologies, Miss Desmond.'

Blair swallowed. 'I'm not apologising,' she said carefully. 'I just... We're both... I mean, this is a stressful situation, and...'

He looked at her coldly. 'Is that right?'

'Look, all I'm trying to do is clear the air, Hunter. I... I'd hate to let that...that little episode between us...'

'Forget about it. I already have.'

'Have you?' Her voice sounded unnaturally sharp, and she cleared her throat. 'Have you?' she repeated. 'Well, I'm glad to hear it, because...'

'It's not worth all this discussion,' he said, easing the car through a tight curve.

'I agree,' she said quickly. 'I just wouldn't want you to get any wrong ideas. I...'

He shrugged his shoulders. 'The little rich girl was out slumming,' he said calmly. 'How could I possibly get the wrong idea about something like that?'

'That's ridiculous, Hunter!'

'Just don't use me in your fantasies any more, OK?'

'Dammit, Hunter, what's that supposed to mean? I don't...'

'Yes, you do,' he said bluntly. 'I don't know exactly what's going on in that beautiful head of yours, but I don't want to be involved in it, do you understand?'

Colour flooded her cheeks. 'I don't want to disappoint you but, once this is over, the only fantasies I'll have about you will be nightmares.'

Hunter grinned mirthlessly. 'That makes two of us. Believe me, Miss Desmond, I've never been so damned eager to get done with a job in my life. I just hope to hell your father tells me what I want to hear.'

Blair took a deep breath and then let it out slowly. 'Yes,' she murmured, 'so do I.'

Suddenly, a road—a real road, she thought, peering through the windscreen—appeared in the distance. Hunter slowed the car as they approached it, although there was no sign of any other traffic. She watched as he checked his mirrors carefully. Finally, he swung on to the macadam surface.

'OK,' he muttered, 'we'll be in Fiorello soon.'

'Fiorello? Is that where we're going?'

'Yes. Fiorello della Montagna—Little Flower of the Mountain, it's called. It's small and well off the major roads.'

'Which makes it safe to take me there.'

Hunter nodded. 'Exactly. But it has a public telephone and a market. You can get a change of clothing, if you need it.' He glanced at her and smiled coolly.

'Nothing you'd find on the Via Veneto, of course, but I'm afraid it's the best I can do.'

'You've been to Fiorello before, then?' Blair asked, ignoring his sarcasm.

'It's the closest town to the farmhouse,' he said.

She was torn between the curious desire to know more about him, and the fear that he'd already told her more than it was healthy for her to know. Finally, curiosity won out.

'Does the farmhouse belong to you?'

'Do you care?' His voice was curt.

'No,' she said stiffly, 'not in the least.'

They rode in silence for another few minutes, and then he turned towards her again. 'Fiorello della Montagna's just down this road a couple of miles,' he said. 'Once we're there, let me do the talking. I don't expect anybody to be looking for us, but it'll be best if no one knows you're American.'

She nodded. There was a field of sunflowers to the left, the stalks so high they rose over the car. On the other side of the narrow road, a herd of goats munched complacently on green grass and summer wildflowers. The road spiralled upwards, dipping and turning as it followed the crest of the mountain, finally curving below a group of tiled-roof buildings clustered around a cobblestoned *piazza*. Colourful stalls ranged around the sides and, even at a distance, Blair could hear the musical babble of voices and laughter.

'This is it,' Hunter said, pulling the Lamborghini beneath the branches of a chestnut tree and pointing up the hill.

'You're kidding,' Blair said softly.

He laughed. 'I told you it was small, didn't I? There's a post office, and a market every week. It's the town's only claim to fame—well, that and the telephone. It counts, too, I suppose.' He swung Blair's door open and reached for her hand. 'Let's go,' he said. 'The sooner we get this over with, the better.'

'My feeling exactly.'

Hunter's eyes met hers and she forced herself not to look away. Finally, he nodded.

'Yes,' he said softly, 'I'm sure it is.'

He slammed the car door and started rapidly up the hill. 'Slow down, will you?' she said as she hurried along beside him. 'Either that, or let go of me.'

'Nice try, Blair.'

'Nice try?' she gasped.

His fingers laced through hers and he drew to a halt. 'Catch your breath. I'll wait. But I'm not going to let go of you.'

She drew a deep gulp of air. 'Don't be paranoid, Hunter. I'm not trying to get away.'

'I'm delighted to hear it,' he said mildly.

'Where would I go? You've got the car keys.'

'Right,' he said smugly, dropping the keys into his pocket. 'Besides,' he added, pulling out a handful of silver coins, 'with a little luck, we'll...damn!'

'What's wrong?'

'I forgot the damned *gettoni*.'

'The what?'

Hunter sighed. 'The *gettoni*. The tokens you need to use a pay phone. Haven't you ever made a call from a public phone in Italy?'

'No,' Blair said with complete honesty, 'I never have.'

He nodded. 'I keep forgetting how the other half lives. You probably never stick that pretty nose out of the Desmond villa, do you?'

'Not often,' she said carefully, praying he wouldn't ask her any questions about Rome.

'And I'll bet you still don't know anything about the real Italy?'

'You could say that, I guess.'

'Yeah,' he said, 'that's what I figured. Well, the tokens aren't a problem. We can buy some at the tobacconist's next to the post office.' Hunter looked at her doubtfully. 'Are you ready for the rest of the climb?'

Blair drew a deep breath. 'I'd climb Mount Everest to make this phone call,' she said.

His face darkened. 'My feelings exactly,' he snapped, and set off at an even more rapid pace.

She fell in beside him. It took two of her steps to match one of his, but there was no sense in asking him to slow down again. Well, of course, he was eager to get the ransom call made so he could trade her for money. And that was fine. The sooner she was safely back in Rome, the better, she thought, crossing the fingers of her free hand. If only the call went well. If only Hunter's demands were reasonable. If only Oscar Desmond agreed to pay. If only...

'Buon giorno.'

Blair looked down in surprise. A small boy was blocking their path, grinning at them both.

'Buon giorno,' Hunter said. *'Come sta?'*

'Va bene,' the boy answered, and from then on Blair was lost. She looked from the child to the man, listening to the swift exchange, watching the animated expressions on both faces, knowing only by the sudden twist of Hunter's mouth and the single, unmistakably English word he uttered that he'd just learned something unpleasant.

'What's the matter?' she whispered. Hunter shook his head and squatted beside the boy. Police? Had the child said 'police'? Her heart began to pound in her ears. He had said it, she was certain. The word sounded almost the same in English as in Italian. Rescue, she thought, but there was no joy in it, only a sudden image of Hunter and blood and pain and...

She bent towards him, her fingers clasping his more tightly. 'Hunter,' she whispered. 'Hunter, please listen to me'

He looked up and frowned. 'I told you to keep still,' he said softly.

'Yes, but...'

The warning glint in his eyes silenced her. She nodded and watched as he turned back to the child. There was another round of rapid Italian, and then Hunter laughed.

'OK,' he said, and the boy stuck his hand into his pocket and pulled out a handful of jingling coins. 'Highway robbery,' Hunter said, handing the child several bills and taking the coins in exchange, but he was smiling while he said it. Finally he stood and ruffled the boy's dark hair. *'Mille Grazie, mio amico,'* he said. *'Ciao.'*

'Prego,' the child grinned. *'Ciao, signor, signorina.'*

'Ciao,' Blair said automatically, staring after him as he skipped down the hill. She looked at Hunter as they began walking again, waiting for him to say something, and finally she cleared her throat. 'Er—Hunter... didn't the boy—I thought he said something about the police.'

'He said the tobacconist's shop was at the top of this hill, but the man who owns it was ill and the shop was closed for the day.'

'And? What does that have to do with the police?'

'I asked the boy if someone else in town sold telephone tokens. At first he said no, but there was a police station nearby and, if we had an urgent call to make, surely they would let me use their telephone.'

'There's a police station here?'

Hunter shrugged. 'Not here, exactly. Just up the road. What's wrong with you, Blair? You're pale as a ghost.'

'I...I just thought...'

'Yeah,' he said gruffly, 'I know what you thought. Well, stop worrying. We'll make that call. The kid is a budding little businessman. It turned out he just happened to have a pocket full of tokens he was willing to sell for twice what they're worth.'

Blair nodded. 'And you bought them.'

'It's a lucky thing we met the little thief,' Hunter laughed. 'I don't know of another phone for miles, and I sure as hell don't want to involve the police. I don't trust them.' He stopped suddenly, and his eyes swept over her face. 'Damn it, Blair, you look terrible. Something *is* the matter. Are you ill? Is it the heat? Here, lean on me.'

She shook her head as his arm slid around her waist. 'I'm ... I'm all right,' she murmured. 'I just ... You're an amazing man, Hunter. Isn't there anything that would stop you from making this call?'

His eyes were expressionless. 'Is that an offer, Miss Desmond?'

She felt a rush of heat suffuse her face. 'Of course it isn't. I just meant...'

'I know what you meant,' he said in a flat, hard voice. 'And you can stop worrying. I told you I'd make the damned call and I will. With any luck at all, we can say goodbye to each other in a couple of hours.'

Blair looked away from him. 'I certainly hope you're right,' she said stiffly.

Minutes later, they were standing in front of an oversized telephone booth that stood in splendid isolation outside a post office that was closed for the midday meal.

'OK,' Hunter said, 'I'll place the call and talk with your old man first. Then I'll hand it over to you.'

Blair nodded nervously. 'Is there ... am I supposed to say anything special?'

He shrugged. 'It doesn't matter to me, Blair. Say whatever you feel like saying. Just don't take all day about it.'

She nodded again. 'I understand. You're afraid they'll trace the call, right?'

'That's not even a possibility. Your father's not a fool. His lines are checked for taps twice a week. I just don't like the idea of being in one place too long. It makes for problems.'

'I see,' she murmured, although she didn't. But, after all, everything she knew about ransom demands came from the movies or television. Didn't the kidnappers always warn the victim not to try and trace their calls? Oscar Desmond would know that; he wouldn't want to do anything to jeopardise her safety.

Her heart thudded as Hunter stepped into the booth and pulled her after him. During the past hours, she had come to believe that Hunter would not hurt her deliberately, but the moment of truth was at hand. Suppose all her assumptions had been wrong? Suppose Desmond refused to pay what Hunter asked? Suppose he told him his captive's true identity? Suppose...

The booth was larger than the ones in the States, but it was still too small to hold the two of them comfortably. No matter how she tried, it was impossible not to lean against him.

'Why don't you let me wait outside? You can leave the door open and hold on to my hand if you don't trust me.'

'I don't trust you at all,' he said curtly. 'Desmond told me you'd try and get away if it ever came to this, and he was right.'

She stared at him in open-mouthed disbelief. 'You mean, you talked about this with him?'

Hunter nodded. 'Believe me, Blair, everything he said about you was true. You're harder to handle than your old man ever dreamed.'

She shook her head as Hunter lifted the receiver. 'But ... but if he knows you, he'll recognise your voice. He'll ...'

Her words tumbled to a halt as he stepped behind her. His arms slid around her, one hand splaying across her hip as he drew her back firmly against him. 'Just keep quiet while I ... good. Now stand still.'

As if she would do anything else, Blair thought, watching while he dropped the tokens into the telephone box. To move would be to court disaster. As it was, she could feel the hard length of Hunter's body pressing against hers, and the warmth of his breath on her cheek. She stole a quick glance at his face. He looked so intent, so determined. What would have happened if they'd met some other way? she wondered suddenly. At a party or a dance or... Would he even have noticed her in a roomful of other women? Probably not, although she'd have noticed him. Hunter would stand out anywhere. Not that it mattered. He wasn't the kind of man she was ever likely to meet again. You didn't stumble across men like Hunter all that often, and to go looking for a man like him was insane...

She turned her face up to his. 'Hunter,' she whispered urgently, 'listen, maybe—maybe you should make this call later. Tomorrow,' she said, ignoring the pounding of her pulse, knowing that what she was saying to him represented surrender. 'Wait until tomorrow...'

But he wasn't listening. The phone was pressed tightly to his ear and he was frowning. 'Quiet!' he barked. 'I can't hear a damned thing.'

Blair touched her fingers lightly to his face. 'Hunter, listen to me, dammit,' she said. 'I won't tell anyone about you. I swear I won't. You don't have to worry. I...'

'Hello,' he said in a clear voice, and then he smiled. 'Yes, Mr Desmond, it's Rhys Hunter. Your daughter is fine. Yes, your daughter.' He laughed politely. 'I don't know why you sound so surprised, Mr Desmond. I told you she'd be safe with me. I will, I'll let you talk to her in a second. I just want to know if it's safe for me to bring her back to Rome yet.' Hunter laughed softly. 'Yeah, you were right, I've had one hell of a time keeping her in sight. She thinks this whole bodyguard thing is some kind of game.'

The floor was tilting beneath Blair's feet. *Rhys?* Was her kidnapper introducing himself? The booth was hot and airless, but that was no reason to hallucinate. And she wasn't hallucinating; she was listening to one end of what seemed to be a perfectly friendly conversation. Hunter was still talking, although she was beyond being able to understand a word he said. Her mind was bouncing like a rubber ball, careening from one unlikely possibility to the next as she tried to come to grips with what had suddenly become reality. Hunter wasn't a kidnapper, he was a bodyguard! She hadn't been abducted, she'd been saved! Oscar Desmond wasn't worried about her, he was relieved she was out of danger. He was telling that to Hunter now, she could tell it from bits and pieces of what Hunter was saying. And Hunter was laughing, damn the man, saying he thought she'd had quite an experience and, yes, Blair was a handful and a half and, by the way, Desmond should have told him his daughter preferred to use her middle name and not her first and... *His daughter?*

'Wait a minute,' Blair cried, grabbing wildly for the telephone. 'Wait just a damned minute...'

Hunter frowned and pulled her back into the tight circle of his arm. 'Your daughter could use some lessons in manners,' he said sharply. 'I guess she heard me say we'll have to stay away for a few more days and she wasn't exactly overjoyed at the possibility. Yes, yes, I understand. All right, here she is. Blair, your father wants to talk to you.' He put his hand over the telephone as he handed it to her. 'Get that look off your face,' he said in a soft growl. 'Believe me, I'm no more thrilled than you are.'

Blair took the receiver from him, her eyes riveted to his face. She put the phone to her ear.

'Hu...hu...' Carefully, she took a deep breath and began again. 'Hello,' she said, still staring at Hunter.

Meryl's breathy whisper made her blink. 'It's me. Blair, please, don't let on. Make believe you're talking to my father. Blair, please, please, listen to me for a second, OK? Just listen...'

'What's the matter?' Hunter asked her. 'Is the line fading?'

Blair shook her head. 'No,' she said finally, 'no, the line's fine. I just...I just...'

'Blair,' Meryl whispered frantically, 'I'll put Daddy on if you'd rather talk to him. Shall I?'

'No,' Blair said slowly, 'I'd much rather talk to you.' She forced a smile to her face and looked up at Hunter. 'Why don't you tell me what's going on back there, *Dad*?'

'Thank you, Blair,' Meryl said. 'Look, I'll make this quick—I guess you're kind of surprised...'

Blair smiled through her teeth. 'Yes, you might say that.'

'Actually, we're surprised, too. We thought you'd have told Mr Hunter who you were. At least, that's what we thought at first...'

'I wish you were here right now, *Daddy*,' Blair said grimly. 'I'd like to see your face while I told you why I didn't. Maybe you can figure it out. Maybe you can imagine how I felt when...'

'Blair, listen, I think I know what happened. I...'

'Do you, *Daddy*?'

'And don't say "Daddy" like that, Blair. You make it sound as if you're angry with me.'

'You're so clever, Dad.'

'All right, I'll get to the point. When we didn't hear from you or Hunter, we began to wonder. I mean, we knew you were probably scared.'

Blair closed her eyes and leaned her forehead against the telephone. 'That's an understatement,' she said hoarsely.

'And Daddy said Mr Hunter is a rather—well—assertive type and that he'd probably be expecting me to be—well—uncooperative.' There was a brief pause and Meryl cleared her throat. 'I usually am, when it comes to security. What I'm getting at is that—well—as the hours ticked by, we guessed that maybe you'd thought you'd been kidnapped and were afraid to tell him who you really were. That's what happened, right?'

Blair nodded. She didn't trust herself to speak, and she only sighed into the phone, but Meryl seemed to understand.

'OK,' Meryl breathed, 'that's what we figured.'

'Blair,' Hunter murmured, 'are you OK?'

She nodded, her head whirling. Two days of terror— and suddenly bits and pieces began to come together. Things Hunter had said about her welfare, about her safety, about her lack of cooperation—things she'd been too naïve or too frightened to understand. Meryl was still talking, urging her to... to what? To go on with the pretence? God, she couldn't! She couldn't...

'It'll just be for a day or two,' Meryl was saying. 'Please, Blair, do it for me. It's just a harmless gag...'

'No!'

'Blair, please—it'll be OK. You'll see.'

Hunter's arm tightened around her. 'Blair,' he whispered, his breath warm against her cheek, 'what's the matter?'

'Noth... nothing,' she said. He's not a criminal, Blair. He's not what you thought he was... You're safe.

'Blair, Jesus, don't pass out on me. Forget the damned phone. Take a deep breath. Come on, that's it. Again...'

Suddenly, the voice whispering into her ear was masculine and authoritative.

'Miss Nolan, this is Oscar Desmond. Listen carefully, young woman. I want you to go on pretending to be my daughter for just a few more days.'

Blair turned as far from Hunter's piercing stare as she could manage. 'No,' she whispered, 'I won't. I...'

'Everyone believes my chauffeur foiled a pair of ambitious paparazzi and whisked Meryl off to a secluded location.'

Hunter's fingers curled around the telephone. 'Let me have that,' he said. 'What the hell's going on? You look like you've seen a ghost.'

'No,' she said quickly. 'I'm fine. I...'

'No one knows Meryl's here, Blair. Her young man and I have been getting acquainted without any disturbances. It's made my daughter very happy.'

'Happy?' Blair whispered. 'Happy? What about me? What about...'

'I've told Hunter it's not safe to come back to the city. He believes me.'

'I don't care about that,' she said in a frantic whisper, trying to turn away from Hunter's piercing stare. 'I don't...'

'I can't tell him the truth. He'd never agree to let me use him as a diversion.'

Blair swallowed drily. 'Yes, but eventually, when the facts are known...'

She could almost hear Desmond shrug. 'I'll worry about it then. Hunter earns a lot of money in my employ. He'll be angry, but I'm sure I can straighten things out.'

Her eyes skimmed over Hunter's face, lingering on his mouth as she remembered the feel of it against her own.

'Do this for Meryl's sake,' Oscar Desmond pleaded.
He wasn't a criminal . . .

'Make it short and sweet, Blair,' Hunter said.

'Yes,' she said to him, 'I will . . .'

But it was Oscar Desmond who answered. 'Good girl,' he rasped, and the phone went dead in her hands.

CHAPTER SEVEN

'WAIT,' said Blair, 'please...'

The drone of the dialling tone mocked her plea. She stared at the receiver and than hung it up slowly, conscious of the sound of Hunter's breathing and the light pressure of his body against hers.

'It's terribly hot in here, Hunter. I need some air...'

She pulled open the door and stumbled out of the booth, drawing deep breaths of the hot, humid air. Her legs felt spongy and everything around her seemed to be losing colour and substance. She made a soft, murmuring sound, and suddenly Hunter's arms closed around her.

'Easy,' he said softly. 'Just lean against me.'

'I'm all right,' she protested, but she lay her head against his chest and closed her eyes, breathing in the heated air as well as the heated scent of his skin.

'That's my girl,' he murmured. One hand moved up to cup the back of her head, lifting the heavy mass of dark curls from the nape of her neck. A hot breeze whispered against her skin, but it felt cool against her damp flesh. 'Better?'

'Yes,' she sighed, her face still pressed against his shirt.

'It's the damned heat,' Hunter said, cradling her against him for a few moments more, then taking her by the shoulders, he moved her gently away from him. 'Let me see...' His eyes scanned her face and he smiled. 'You'll be fine. We'll get you something cool to drink at the market. I should have realised the weather would affect you. It takes time to get used to it.'

'It's not that,' she said, and then she stopped. She'd almost told him that Iowa was a lot worse than this in midsummer, and what a mistake that would have been. What would Meryl Desmond know about Iowa, in midsummer or any other time?

'Don't argue with me, Blair,' he said, looping his arm around her waist. 'I've seen heat-stroke before. Pale face, clammy skin—just the way you looked when you stepped out of that booth. Let's get some liquids into you, and then get you something lighter than those trousers and that sweater. And you need a hat to keep the sun off your head. You'll be OK,' he said, starting down the hill with her tucked firmly against him. 'There's nothing to worry about.'

No, there wasn't, she thought, walking along obediently beside him. Well, there was. She had to keep pretending she was Meryl or tell Hunter the truth, and she wasn't about to do that, not until she had things sorted out. Desmond had said Hunter would be angry if he knew he was being deceived. She glanced up at him and thought of the intensity with which he'd guarded her the past two days. Yes, she thought, he probably would be angry—and at her. It was always the messenger who brought the bad news who lost his head. And then would come Meryl's tears and Oscar Desmond's anger—cooler than Hunter's, but anger none the less—and before she knew it she'd be unemployed and broke and . . .

That was the bad news. Now for the plus side of the situation. The terror of the past couple of days was over. Hunter wasn't a desperado. God, it was crazy! She wanted to laugh and cry and . . . He wasn't a kidnapper at all, although who could blame her for not being able to tell the difference? It wasn't every day you were snatched off the street and tossed into a car. Or hustled half-way across a foreign country by a tight-lipped madman. Or treated without the slightest bit of human decency...

She stumbled over a cobblestone and Hunter's arm caught her closer to him. How solicitous he was being, she thought, glancing up at him. Not that it was the first time. That was the way he'd been all along. Concerned one minute and cruel the next. No, not cruel exactly. Cold. Contemptuous. Yes, that was a good way to describe his behaviour, especially when he'd humiliated her, degraded her... which he'd done as often as he possibly could. *Hunter, you bastard!*

Blair pulled free of his arm. 'I can walk by myself, thank you,' she said, her words like ice.

His eyes met hers. 'Feeling better, I see.'

There was something in his voice... Her head swung up and she glared at him, but his face mirrored only polite concern. Too polite, she thought. He was mocking her, damn him! She could see it in his eyes. Deep within himself, he was laughing at her, just as he had last night when she'd asked him to stop at a ladies' room, and this morning when she'd asked for her shoes...

He's a bully, Blair. And you've played right into his hands... But not any more. He was... he was nothing but an employee, when you came right down it it. A bodyguard. Muscle, and not much else. And there wasn't a damned thing to be afraid of, not from now on.

She waited while he unlocked the car, and then she turned her back on him. 'Get me something cold to drink,' she said over her shoulder. 'Make sure there's plenty of ice in it.'

The laughter was visible on his face, now, tugging at his mouth. 'Anything you say, Miss Desmond.'

Blair's hands went to her hips. 'That's right,' she said. 'Anything I say. Just see you remember that, Hunter.'

'One call to Daddy and we turn into a tiger,' he said softly. 'Interesting.'

'You have put me through a very difficult couple of days, Hunter. I just wanted you to know that things are going to be different from now on.'

One of his eyebrows rose lazily. 'Really?' he said, as if she'd told him something amazing.

Blair pushed her hair back from her face. 'Yes, really. We may have to stay away from Rome for another day or two...'

'At least.'

'...but you're not going to push me around any more. Is that understood?'

'I haven't pushed you around, Blair. I've merely done what was necessary for your safety.'

Blair uttered a quick, unladylike retort and he laughed. A blush rose to her cheeks, not because of what she'd said, but because of the way he'd reacted to it. *That damned contemptuous attitude of his again...*

'My, my, how quickly we revert to type,' he said.

'There's nothing funny about this,' she hissed. 'I'm angry, Hunter. Damned angry! And I just want to make sure you... What are you doing? Hunter, stop that! Let me go...'

It was useless. She might as well not have been talking. He scooped her up, swung open the car door, and tossed her into the seat as easily as he had the first time at the airport. She was still sputtering as he got in, stuck the key into the ignition and turned on the airconditioning.

'Relax,' he said easily, 'and cool off a little, Blair. The heat seems to have gone to your head.'

'How dare you?' she said, her voice shaking with barely restrained fury. 'I was talking to you, Hunter, and when I talk, you'd damn well better list——'

He was on her in an instant, his hands clasping her wrists, his face inches from hers. She caught her breath at the cold fire burning in his eyes.

'Listen, Miss Desmond,' he growled, 'I don't know what's got you so fired up, but if that's what happens to you after one talk with Daddy, you can forget about any others until we get back to Rome.'

'Don't talk to me that way, Hunter. Who do you think you are? Who...'

'I'm the man who holds your life in my hands,' he said. 'And I'll talk to you any damned way I please.'

'You do not hold my life in your hands,' she said furiously. 'You're my bodyguard, not my kidnapper. The game's over, Hunter. I'm not afraid of you any more.'

He stared at her for a moment, and then a look of incredulity spread across his face.

'Your kidnapper?' His eyes searched hers and he began to chuckle. 'You're not serious!'

'I am not going to discuss it,' she said, refusing to look at him.

'I don't believe it,' he said, laughing softly. 'You thought I...? Is that why you tried so damned hard to get away from me?'

'Anyone would try and get away from you, Hunter,' she said coldly. 'I'm sure that's not news to a man like you.'

To her surprise, the laughter fled from his face. 'You're right,' he said in clipped tones. 'It's not. And that only makes me more attuned to every trick you can think of, Miss Desmond. I suggest you keep that in mind before you try any more funny business.'

Blair turned to stare at him and then she slammed her fist against the dashboard. 'Why in God's name didn't you tell me who you were?' she demanded.

Hunter shrugged his shoulders. 'I did. I gave you my name—didn't your father tell you I'd be picking you up at the airport?'

'I...I was told you were a new chauffeur, not a bodyguard.'

'Maybe Desmond didn't want to upset you by telling you anything else.'

'Anything else??'

'We got word that someone might try a snatch the night before you were due in Rome.'

Blair's eyes widened. 'You mean...those men who tried to hustle me into the Fiat weren't paparazzi?'

Hunter gave her a grim smile. 'Good thinking, Miss Desmond. But they're off our backs. Your father told me the police picked them up minutes after we got away. That's not the story the papers got, of course. Desmond followed my recommendations; my policy is never to publicise these damned attempted kidnappings. Publicity's half the reason they take place.'

'He followed your what?'

'My recommendations. My firm provides security for Desmond Enterprises in Europe.' His eyes swept over her and he gave her a cold smile. 'You were most vulnerable from the airport to the villa. If they were going to make a try for you, I figured it would be then. So I decided to swap places with the chauffeur. I didn't want to take any chances on your doing something stupid, like disappearing for a quick swim at Capri. Your reputation's preceded you, Miss Desmond. Everybody from your old man down to that poor son of a bitch you lost last winter had warned me that it was impossible to provide you with proper security.'

Meryl, you just wait until I get my hands on you...

'Why don't you tell me about it?' Blair asked carefully. 'I'd love to hear your version of what happened.'

'Let's not play games, Blair,' Hunter growled. 'You slipped away from him every chance you got during the month you were here. That's why he lost the account; it's what convinced your father that he couldn't afford not to hire the best.' He leaned across the console towards her and she drew in her breath. 'It's why I've anticipated

every trick you tried to pull. Just remember that. As
long as you're in Italy, I'll be as close to you as your
skin.'

Blair swallowed, and drew back from the intense
expression in Hunter's eyes.

'You... you didn't have to treat me the way you did,'
she murmured.

'I did what had to be done to keep you safe,' he said.

'You... you terrorised me...'

Hunter laughed softly. 'How the hell was I supposed
to know you thought I'd abducted you?'

'Look, Mr Hunter...'

'Rhys,' he said softly, and then he grinned. 'Surely
we're on a first name basis after all we've shared, Blair.'

She felt a swift rush of heat flood her cheeks. 'My—
my father said you'd tell me why we can't go back to
Rome just yet.'

Hunter sighed and sank back in the leather seat.
'Nothing terribly serious, Blair. There have been labour
problems at your father's mills, and—well, sometimes
people have strange ideas about the negotiating process.
Your father and I agreed that it might be best if you
didn't become a bargaining chip.'

Blair caught her bottom lip between her teeth. 'Don't
you have... don't you have things to do back in Rome?'
she asked hesitantly. 'I mean, if you're the head of security for my... my father... Couldn't you send one of
your men to take over for you here?'

'Yes,' he said curtly, 'I'm sure we'd both prefer that.
And you're right—I have any number of things to do.
I provide security for several corporations. But Desmond
is the only one that has trouble now.'

She took a deep breath. 'Then we'd better get some
things straightened out, Hunter,' she said carefully.

'Let me guess,' he said sarcastically. 'You just have
to stay at the Excelsior in Florence. My Lamborghini

gets swapped for a Mercedes. And you simply must do some shopping on the Via Tornabuoni and the Ponte Vechhio.'

Blair drew herself up. 'I want you to remember your function, *Mister* Hunter. You're here to protect me, and that's fine—as far as it goes. It doesn't mean you have the right to bully me or humiliate me or...'

'Oh,' he said softly, 'you want to discuss the rules, is that right?'

'Yes,' she said, 'exactly. I...'

'There's only one rule, Blair.' His voice was surprisingly gentle. 'If you value your life, you'll do what I tell you to do. That's the first rule, the last rule, the only rule. Dammit, Blair,' he yelled as she grabbed the handle and wrenched the door open, 'where the hell are you going?'

Where, indeed? she thought grimly as her feet hit the ground. But enough was enough. If Rhys Hunter really thought she was going to go on taking orders from him, he was crazy! Two days of all but clicking her heels each time the man barked a command was more than enough for anybody. He was her bodyguard, dammit, not her captor! He was her employee, when you came right down to it. Well, he would have been if she were really Meryl Desmond. And Meryl certainly wouldn't put up with being treated like a...a chattel, she thought indignantly as she hurried across the *piazza*. Let him get used to the idea that she gave the orders around here. Let him...

She gasped as his hand caught her elbow. 'Let go,' she said through clenched teeth.

'You're making a scene,' he said quietly, pulling her tightly against his side. 'People are staring at us.'

She looked up, noticing the faces watching them for the first time. 'Let them,' she grunted, trying to pull free of his hand. 'If it embarrasses you, that's just too bad.'

'Will you stop being such a damned spoiled brat?' he growled. 'Do you want someone to begin asking questions about you?'

'Yes,' she snapped, tripping along beside him as he marched her through the market stalls. 'I'll tell them you're mistreating me. I'll tell them . . .'

'What?' he rasped in her ear. 'That you're Meryl Desmond? Meryl Desmond is literally worth her weight in gold to some of these people.'

A tremor of apprehension beat in Blair's throat. 'You're just trying to frighten me,' she said quickly. 'These are honest people . . .'

'Most of them, sure. But all we'd need is one who's not. Or one radical lunatic who wants to make a statement.' He bent his head to hers. 'Kidnapping is as political as it is economic these days,' he whispered.

His breath was warm against her ear, but what he'd said made her shiver. She knew just enough about the insanity of the world to know he was probably right. And she also knew that what she'd gone through since yesterday would pale beside the real thing. Her footsteps slowed, and she slumped against him in defeat as they reached the end of the market.

'All right,' she said wearily, 'you've made your point. I'll behave.'

He nodded. 'You're damned right you will.'

'Hunter, look, I promise, I'll do as you say.'

He eyed her narrowly. 'Until the next time.'

Blair sighed. 'No,' she said, 'until we return to Rome.' His hands clasped her shoulders and he turned her towards him. She lifted her face and her eyes met his. 'It was bad enough being kidnapped by my own bodyguard,' she said in a voice that was supposed to be light. 'I don't think I'd have survived the real thing . . .'

To her horror, her voice trembled and broke. What had begun as laughter ended as a sob. Hunter cursed softly, and his hands slid up her throat and cupped her face.

'Blair...'

She waved her hands between them and shook her head. She wanted to tell him she was fine, but the words wouldn't come. Only tears came, streaming down her face. He gathered her against him, holding her while she cried, until finally she drew away and ran the back of her hand across her nose.

'You can't im-imagine what I thought,' she said, laughing and crying at the same time. 'Especially last night, when you...when you...'

'You told me you'd try and get away, dammit.' Hunter shook his head. 'And I needed some rest—we both did. I didn't know what would be facing us today.'

'Yes,' she said, 'it all makes sense—now. But last night, I...I...'

'Jesus, Blair, I'm here to protect you, not hurt you.'

This time, she managed something that was close to a smile. 'It wasn't your fault, Hunter. I just put two and two together and came up with five. I mean, you're right—you did tell me who you were. You had no way of knowing Mer...my father hadn't told me to expect you. In fact, now that I think about it, everything you said was really supposed to make me feel better.' Blair sniffed again. 'Do you know that I'm leaking all over your shirt?' she asked with a shaky laugh. 'I'm using you like a giant tissue.'

Hunter pulled a handkerchief from his pocket and put it to her nose. 'Blow,' he said.

She did, noisily, and then she smiled at him. 'I feel so stupid. How could I have misunderstood everything you said? I heard it all, but...'

'Did you? I said a hell of a lot of things, Blair. And I did a lot of things...'

'You don't owe me an apology, Hunter. It was just a terrible misunderstanding, that's all.'

He took the handkerchief from her and moved closer to her. 'You didn't let me finish,' he said softly, dabbing at her damp eyes. 'I'm sorry you were frightened. But I'm not sorry for the things I did. I'd do them again, if I had to. My job is to keep you safe. If that means tying you up, I will. If it means locking you inside the car, I will. If it means taking away your clothes...'

Her eyes slid quickly from his. 'Hunter, please...'

'Blair, listen,' he said roughly, his hands cupping her face and lifting it to his. 'I'll do whatever I have to do to take care of you. Do you understand?'

'Yes,' she said. 'That's why I said it was a misunderstanding. If I'd known what you were really doing, I wouldn't have tried to get away.'

He smiled into her eyes. 'That's not the way I've heard it.'

'Look, you heard wrong. I'm not like that. Meryl...' Meryl would behave that way, not I, she'd almost said. And it was true. Hadn't Meryl got a kick out of deceiving the reporters that day in Los Angeles? Hadn't she dreamed up the whole Customs caper? Lord only knew what she'd done in the past... 'Meryl Blair Desmond isn't a dummy, you know.'

His smile widened. 'No, she's not. In fact, she's not anything like I thought she would be.'

Blair's heart thumped against her ribs. *Be careful*, she thought, but it was impossible not to ask him the first thing that danced into her mind.

'Is that good or bad?'

His thumbs stroked the smooth skin across her cheekbones. 'What do you think?' he said softly.

Blair smiled. 'I think it proves you should never believe everything you hear.'

His eyes glinted with laughter. 'Including your promise to behave yourself?'

'You have to learn to discriminate between what's true and what's not, Hunter,' she laughed. 'Would a woman who's just told you she spent the past couple of days in fear for her life want to put herself in that position again? Believe me, I've had enough of being kidnapped to last me a lifetime.'

Hunter's eyes searched hers. 'You weren't always afraid, Blair,' he said softly.

Her blood seemed to grow thick in her veins. There was no need to ask him what he meant, no point in trying to play coy. He was remembering the times he'd kissed her, the times his touch had ignited a passion so intense it had been frightening.

'No,' she said finally, the word a sigh. 'I wasn't.'

His eyes darkened as he moved closer to her. 'I want to believe you,' he said huskily.

'Believe me, Hunter,' she whispered. 'I won't run away.'

His eyes searched hers. 'If I trust you and you let me down...'

'Yes?' she whispered.

He smiled, but it wasn't a smile like any she'd ever seen before. 'We'd both regret it.'

The hot August air was so still that she could hear the sound of her own breathing. His words hung between them, and suddenly she wondered when they had stopped talking about his role as her bodyguard. Whatever they'd been saying to each other these past minutes, it had nothing to do with that kind of trust. But it had to. That was what this was all about, wasn't it? He was Rhys Hunter and she—she was supposed to be Meryl Desmond, she was supposed to be...

If I trust you and you let me down...

Suddenly, she knew she had to tell him the truth about herself. Now, she thought, before it was too late, before there was no turning back.

'Hunter,' she whispered, but the rest of the words caught in her throat. She was drowning, drowning in the silver flames that burned deep within his eyes.

'Come here,' he murmured. His hands moved to the back of her head, his fingers threading into her hair as he drew her to him. Blair lifted her face to his, her eyes half closed, and he bent towards her and touched his mouth lightly to hers. It was a sweet kiss that lasted no longer than a heartbeat, but she felt the heat of his passion flame through her. His tongue touched hers in a gentle caress, searing her with the sweetness of his mouth, and then it was over. His hands closed on her shoulders and he put her gently away from him.

She swayed unsteadily for an instant, and then her eyes opened. Hunter was smiling at her in a way that made her heart turn over. Blair put her hand to her mouth and touched her fingers to her lips.

'All right,' he said softly. 'We've made our bargain and sealed it.'

'Hunter...'

She gasped as something butted her lightly in the ribs. A donkey with a straw hat perched cockily between its long ears shoved its head between them. Hunter laughed as the animal brayed.

'I guess this guy is trying to tell us he witnessed our pact,' he said, running his hand along its velvet muzzle. 'Right, boy?'

The donkey brayed again and Blair smiled. 'What *she's* trying to tell us is that you promised me something cool to wear. Something like this charming hat, for instance.'

Hunter smiled and clasped her hand in his. 'Come on,' he said. 'We may have to go through the whole market, but we're not leaving Fiorello until we find a hat like our pal's. I promise.'

CHAPTER EIGHT

BLAIR hummed softly as she padded from the scarred wooden table to the sink. Late afternoon sunlight filled the farmhouse kitchen, washing the profusion of fruits and vegetables that spilled across the table-top with soft orange hues. The warbling notes of a songbird drifted through the open door, softening the clash of metal on metal, sounds which accompanied the occasional muttered curses coming from beneath the raised bonnet of the Lamborghini.

She added a handful of white mushrooms to the mounded vegetables in the sink and then pumped in a stream of cold water. She could make ratatouille, she thought idly. That was, if Hunter liked it . . .

If Hunter liked it. The thought was so incongruous that it brought her to a complete stop. A few hours ago, what Hunter liked wouldn't have mattered a damn. It still seemed impossible to believe that one simple telephone call had changed so much. But it had, of course. It had changed everything.

God, but it was hot! She brushed the back of her hand across her brow. Lemonade, she thought suddenly. Lemonade had always been her aunt's favourite summertime remedy against the heat. And they'd bought lemons and sugar at the market in Fiorello. Hunter would like lemonade—everybody did. And he had to be parched by now. He'd been peering into the car ever since they'd returned more than an hour ago, the back seat of the Lamborghini laden with produce and groceries and a change of clothing for each of them, all of it topped off by the straw hat Hunter had bought her. Its brim was so broad that it had been impossible to wear it in the car. But he'd been right, it had kept her cooler, and they'd both laughed at the sight of her in it. Blair couldn't remember the last time she'd enjoyed an afternoon as much.

A shadow fell across the room and she looked up. Hunter stood in the doorway, bare to the waist. There were dark smears on his jeans, and a narrow striping of oily dirt ran over the bridge of his nose and across his cheeks. His face and torso were shiny with sweat.

'Nine million degrees Fahrenheit,' he gasped, leaning against the door frame, 'and that damned car decides to contract a terminal disease.'

'Did you find out what's wrong with it?'

He sighed. 'I'm not certain,' he said, wiping his forearm across his eyes. 'It's either the torsion bar or the ball joints—all I'm sure of is that something's wrong with the suspension.' He took the glass Blair held out to him and smiled gratefully. 'Thanks. I feel as if I've just crossed the Sahara.' She watched as he tossed down the contents. 'Good God, woman, was that lemonade?' he demanded, as a pleased smile spread across his face.

She smiled. 'Good?'

'Good? Perfect is more like it. There are some things you just can't get anywhere but back home. Real hot dogs. Popcorn with just the right amount of butter.' He grinned and held the glass out to her. 'Lemonade that tastes like California and Florida rolled into one. Is there more?'

She laughed as she refilled his glass. 'The compliment's lovely, but the lemons are Italian.'

Hunter gulped down half a glass and then smiled at her. 'But the woman who made it is American,' he said. 'That makes the difference.'

The simple compliment pleased her beyond reason, and she turned away in confusion. 'So,' she said briskly, 'what do we do now? Can you fix the car?'

He shook his head. 'No way. It needs a garage and a lift and a hell of a lot more expertise than I have. The worst of it is that it's my own damned fault—I should have figured that taking these roads at high speed would be too much to ask of a car like the Lamborghini.' Hunter put the glass down on the table and gestured at the vegetables in the sink. 'Can you take that stuff out of the sink so I can wash?'

'Sure—just let me get that bowl . . . OK, it's all yours.'

'Thanks.' She watched as he pumped the handle until a stream of water poured from the spigot. Then he closed his eyes, took a breath, and ducked his head under the water.

'God, that's cold!' he gasped.

Blair laughed. 'But good for you, my Aunt Annie used to say.'

Hunter cocked his head and looked up at her from beneath his thatch of dark, wet hair.

'Now, what would a Desmond know about cold water pumped from a well?' he asked with a grin.

Nothing, Blair thought desperately, but she managed a quick smile. 'You'd be surprised,' she said with offhand indifference. 'Aunt Annie was the black sheep of the family. Nobody talks about her much.'

He laughed as he bent over the sink again and let the water pour down on his head and shoulders. 'Ah, I see. Well, every family's entitled to one, I guess. Hand me the soap, will you?'

She did as he asked, then leaned back against the table, arms folded across her chest, watching as he lathered his face and neck. That was close, Blair, she thought. You almost forgot the part you're playing. You almost told him you know all about pumps and wells, about the spring house...

How many hours had she spent during her lonely childhood, playing within its cool stone walls? The spring house stood near the wood pile, behind the farmhouse in Iowa, a relic of simpler times and tastes. It was hardly ever used now, but it still contained a working pump that brought up the coldest, clearest water Blair had ever tasted. Even Aunt Annie preferred it to what came out of the stainless steel spigots in the kitchen, although Uncle Edgar insisted the water was exactly the same. It didn't taste the same, though. It tasted of dark, underground caverns and chill streams, just as this water did. And it had made lemonade that tasted almost the same...

'Is there a towel somewhere?' She blinked slowly and focused her eyes on Hunter. 'You were a million miles away,' he said softly. 'You looked so contented that I almost hated to call you back.'

Blair smiled as she handed him a rough length of linen she'd found in one of the kitchen drawers.

'I was thinking how nice it is here,' she said, watching as he brought the towel to his face. 'This is a wonderful old house. These stone walls must have seen generations of life.'

Hunter peered at her over the edge of the towel. 'Wonderful old house? Last night it was a—what did you call it? A hovel, wasn't it?'

'I didn't mean it. The house just seemed ominous.' She paused. 'So did you.'

'But not today.'

She shook her head and smiled. 'Not today,' she said.

She watched as he dried himself, her eyes following the towel as he rubbed it briskly across his face and down his neck. He had a strong, well proportioned body that he accepted with a natural grace. Droplets of water gleamed in the fine, dark covering of hair on his chest.

His pectorals were well defined, as were his biceps, and his abdomen was flat and ridged with muscle. She wondered if he worked out with weights or ran to keep in shape. Everybody did, back in LA. But Hunter wasn't everybody. He was, in fact, like no one she'd ever known. He was . . .

'Did I miss a spot of grease?' he asked in a soft, teasing voice.

The colour rose to her face. 'Sorry,' she said quickly, turning away from his amused expression. 'I . . . I was thinking about the . . . the car and what you said about not being able to use it.'

'I didn't say we couldn't use it,' he said in a voice gone suddenly cool. 'Don't worry, Blair. We're not stuck out here.'

'I didn't mean that, Hunter,' she said quickly, 'I . . .'

He sighed and tossed the towel across a chair. 'Forget it,' he said evenly. 'I didn't mean to bite your head off. I'm just ticked at myself for not realising I would need something with four-wheel drive in country like this.' His voice grew muffled as he picked up his shirt and slipped it over his head. 'We can drive the Lamborghini, but damned slowly. What we'll do is take it into Florence tomorrow, bring it to a garage, and see about hiring a Land Rover or a Safari or . . .'

'Florence?' she asked, spinning around to face him. 'Really?'

Hunter laughed. 'Really.'

'Oh, that's nice,' she said happily. 'I've always wanted to see Florence.'

'Come on, Blair, you're not going to tell me you've never been there.'

She'd done it again. Of course Meryl had been to Florence. Well, she didn't know it for certain, but Meryl had been everywhere. *Think, Blair, think . . .* What had Meryl said about the Desmonds?

'The Desmonds came from Italy three generations ago,' she said with a forced smile. 'Our name was Di Simondi then. My father says...he says they could never have afforded to live in Rome then, so now he gets a special pleasure out of reversing history. As far as he's concerned, Italy begins and ends in Rome.'

Hunter pulled a chair from the table, turned it around and straddled it. 'Yes, that sounds like something he'd say.' He folded his arms along the top of the chair back and looked at her. 'You're not anything like him, you know. In fact, sometimes, when you talk about your father, you sound as if you're talking about a stranger.'

Careful, she thought, *careful*... 'We're just different, that's all.'

'Yeah, but it's more than that. It's...'

'We haven't spent much time together. You know, he's got business interests everywhere. He travels a lot.'

'And your mother died when you were just a kid.'

She nodded. That, at least, was true. It was a strange bond she and Meryl shared. 'There was a car accident...' Her voice trailed off. The accident had taken her father from her, too, but she couldn't tell him that, although suddenly she wanted to. She wanted to tell him how lonely and frightened she'd been when Aunt Annie and Uncle Edgar came for her. 'It...it was hard.'

Hunter nodded. 'I can imagine.'

'I know it sounds silly, but it took a long time until I stopped waiting for her to come back. Of course, I was very little...'

He shrugged. 'I never waited,' he said in a flat voice. 'My mother left me when I was seventeen, but I'd been expecting it for years.'

Blair looked up in surprise. It was the first personal thing he'd told her about himself.

'It wasn't an accident, you mean? Was she sick?'

His laughter was sharp. 'In a way, it was a little of each, I guess. Actually, *I* was the accident.'

'What do you mean?'

He gave her an artificial smile. 'I was a statistic. You know, X number of babies born to X number of un-married, teenage mothers. And this was a lot of years ago, Blair, when having babies without benefit of wedlock wasn't something every Hollywood celebrity was doing.'

Blair slid into the chair opposite him. 'Not so many years,' she said softly.

He smiled again. 'Thirty-four years,' he said. 'And sometimes it feels more like ten times that.'

'And your mother got sick?'

'What she got was sick of being saddled with a kid which she'd never wanted in the first place,' he said gruffly. 'So she just walked out.'

Blair waited for him to say something more. 'And?' she asked finally, her eyes on his face. 'What did you do?'

Hunter's eyes met hers. 'I learned a valuable lesson,' he said flatly. 'If you don't take care of yourself, nobody else will.'

'You don't mean that!'

His lips drew back from his teeth in a mirthless smile. 'The hell I don't.'

'But you were just a kid. There must have been someone...'

'Yes,' he said, still smiling that strange smile, 'there was. The woman who owned the rooming house we lived in. She was all heart. She said the rent on the room was paid for the next two months, and after that...' He shrugged his shoulders. 'Hell, I hated that damned place anyway. It was cold in the winter and hot in the summer.' The smile crinkled the corners of his eyes. 'And we had a terrific view of back yards filled with clotheslines. Not exactly the style to which you're accustomed, is it?'

'No,' she said, remembering the Iowa farm, 'no, I guess not.'

'Well, it was all there was... Anyway, my mother didn't exactly abandon me. She waited until I was in my last year of high school—I mean, hell, she'd been threatening to take off since my twelfth birthday.' He shoved back his chair and got to his feet. 'She left a note and a fifty-dollar bill in the sugar bowl. The note said she hoped I'd understand...'

He was standing at the sink, his back to her. Blair ached to go to his side, to reach out and touch him, but there was something in the set of his spine that warned her not to do anything but listen. She waited for him to speak again; when he didn't, she cleared her throat.

'But—you were only seventeen...'

'Hell,' he said, letting out his breath, 'it wasn't the end of the world. I stayed until the rent was due, looking for a way to get by. There wasn't any, of course, so finally I took a bus to the nearest Army recruitment office and enlisted.'

'Don't you have to be eighteen to enlist in the Army? What about the authorities? What...'

Hunter laughed softly. 'There are always ways around the rules, Blair. I lied about my age—I think my recruiting officer knew, but Nam was eating up as many guys as they could send, and nobody was asking too many questions.'

'Is that where they sent you? To Viet Nam?' He nodded, and she waited for him to say something, but he remained silent, his expression unreadable. 'Was it—I've read things, heard things... Was it bad?'

The soft sound of his laughter made the hair rise on the back of her neck. 'Bad doesn't do it justice. It was like finding yourself in the bowels of Hell.' He was facing her now but not looking at her, his eyes dark with memory, his face taut with pain. 'Did you ever have a nightmare, know you were having it, but you couldn't wake up? Well, that's what Viet Nam was like.'

'But you could have told them you were under age,' she said. 'You could have told them you'd lied. The Army shouldn't have done that to you. They...'

His head came up sharply. 'The Army took a scared, skinny kid who had nothing, and made him a man, Blair. They taught him about honour and trust, something that didn't exist in the world he came from.' A grim smile twisted his mouth. 'Hell, my honour was all I had. When you come right down to it, it's all anybody has.'

'But there were extenuating circumstances...'

'There are no extenuating circumstances, not when it comes to integrity.'

If I trust you and you let me down... She remembered his words. They echoed and re-echoed through her mind.

'Hunter,' she said, 'sometimes—there are things...' Her voice trembled and broke. *Stop it,* she told herself sharply. Only her guilt had turned what he'd said into an accusation. 'I just meant that there are times you have to bend a little. Things aren't always black and white. Sometimes—sometimes there are reasons...'

'Reasons? Excuses, you mean. Alibis.'

He drew in his breath and turned away from her, tension knotting the muscles in his shoulders and back.

'Rhys?' she whispered.

'Jesus,' he murmured, 'it must be the heat.' He laughed uncomfortably. 'I don't usually try to bore people to death with the story of my life.'

Blair shook her head. 'It...it wasn't boring,' she said quickly. 'I just wish...Rhys, I wish...'

Hunter turned towards her. 'I like the way you say that.' His voice was suddenly soft.

'What?'

He looked into her eyes and smiled. 'Rhys,' he said. 'I've been called "Hunter" for so many years I'd almost forgotten I had another name.'

Blair took a breath. 'It's...it's a nice name. It has a sound that I...'

Her words tumbled into a hot silence that was accentuated by the buzzing of a honeybee as it hovered outside the window. It was Hunter who finally looked away.

'So,' he said, clearing his throat, 'what's for dinner?'

'Dinner?' she repeated foolishly. It was the last thing she'd expected him to say.

'Or don't poor little rich girls know how to cook?'

'I don't know about poor little rich girls,' Blair said softly. 'But if you're asking me if *I* can cook, the answer is yes.'

'Great,' he said with a tired smile, 'I'm bushed.'

He did look tired, she realised suddenly. There were dark shadows beneath his eyes, and the lines around his mouth seemed to have deepened.

'You'll feel better after some ratatouille,' she said. 'We have everything we need...'

'Ratawhat?' He laughed and held his hands up in surrender. 'Listen, Blair, I spent almost half my life soldiering in places where people eat things you don't even want to dream about. One simple rule got me through. I never eat anything I can't pronounce.'

The tension had eased from his face, and she breathed a silent prayer to whatever gods had made her name something like ratatouille to a man who probably thought anything but meat and potatoes was exotic.

'It's a French vegetable stew made from aubergine and tomatoes and onions and...' She chuckled at the expression of disbelief that spread across his face. 'Don't look that way, Rhys. It's delicious, really.'

'The French name was bad enough, but the English description is even worse. Vegetable stew?' He shuddered. 'No, thanks, Miss Desmond. I'll make us some eggs and...'

'You'll like this,' Blair said firmly, handing him a knife. 'Just sit down and start peeling those onions.'

Rhys sighed and dropped into the seat opposite her. 'Well, what the hell. I'll try anything once—where did you learn to make this stuff? The cordon bleu school?'

She laughed as she sliced into a mushroom. 'The *Good Housekeeping Cookbook*. Slice the onions thinly, please, and put them in this bowl.'

He nodded. They worked in companionable silence for a few minutes, the only sound the faint trills of the birds outside the window and the occasional soft whisper of the hot summer breeze. Blair glanced across the table. Rhys was frowning with concentration as he sliced an onion with what seemed to be surgical precision. Just this morning, she'd been scared half to death of this man, and now they were preparing a meal together. A flush of pleasure crept over her skin.

'What are you thinking?' he asked, smiling at her. 'You look like the cat that just swallowed the cream.'

'I...I was just wondering...' She swallowed drily. 'How did you get into the bodyguarding business, anyway? I don't suppose they teach it in college.'

He gave her a quick smile. 'They teach it in the Army. Some of it, anyway, especially in Special Forces.' She looked at him blankly and he shrugged. 'The Green Berets.'

Blair grinned as she popped a mushroom into her mouth. 'John Wayne, hmm?'

Rhys laughed. 'Yeah, something like that. Anyway, Security was a growing field when I got out. So I took my back pay and sunk it into the rent on a one-room office on the Paseo del Prado in Madrid.'

Her eyebrows rose. 'Pretty exotic address for a former soldier, Mr Hunter.'

'I wasn't exactly a soldier,' he said, looking at the knife. 'Anyway, Madrid seemed as good a place as any. There was some heavy stuff going down and I had some contacts...' He shrugged. 'Things went well for me and, within a few years, we expanded to four countries and six offices.'

'And you're still modest and self-effacing.'

He grinned. 'Actually, I'm still amazed.'

Blair sighed. 'I suppose it says something about the world we live in. Lots of people need bodyguards, don't they?'

'We're security specialists, Blair. I'm not minimising the need for bodyguards—sometimes there's nothing that can replace that kind of thing.'

'Like now?'

'Exactly. But the field has become very sophisticated. It...' His eyes narrowed. 'Daddy's kept you pretty far from the realities of life, hasn't he?'

Blair rose quickly and dumped the cut-up vegetables into a pot. 'I...I don't know much about all this, I guess.'

'Well, I can't blame him. Some of it isn't pleasant. Still, if you knew something about the political crazies in this world, or the kind of industrial warfare that goes on, you wouldn't have treated your security so casually in the past.' He stood and crossed the room towards her. 'Here, let me get that started,' he said, taking the box of wooden matches from her hand. 'There's a knack to it...' He bent over the stove and poked at the kindling until a tiny flame sprang up. Then he took the pot from her. 'In fact,' he said, setting it on the grate, 'if you hadn't had such a bad reputation, I wouldn't have given this job my personal attention.'

Blair smiled. 'Your personal attention? Somehow, I can't picture you seated at a desk.'

He chuckled softly. 'No, neither can I. I spend as much time as I can in the field. But I don't do much of this sort of work. My clients are mostly American corporations with European interests and a penchant for privacy. That means I get to play with some very pricey electronic toys.'

'You mean you install those cameras I see mounted in banks?'

Hunter's teeth flashed whitely. 'I mean we sweep boardrooms and bedrooms for bugs the size of pinheads. We install homing devices no bigger than that in cars. We snug sonar scanners and infra-red scanners into dark corners. We...'

'Good grief!' she laughed. 'It sounds like James Bond.'

'Or the CIA,' he said softly.

She looked at him in amazement. 'You're kidding.'

He shook his head. 'The Company recruited some of us in Nam. I guess they decided I was...good at what I did. Anyway, they offered me a job.' Hunter laughed softly. 'God, I'm doing it again! What is it about you that makes me open up like a bad novel?'

Blair smiled. 'Don't stop now,' she said. 'I'm fascinated. I've never known anyone who was a spy before.'

He grinned at her. 'The Company frowns on the use of that word.'

'Did you really go to work for them?'

He nodded. 'Yeah, I did. At first, it was pretty heady stuff. I was still just a kid, full of idealism and some vision of the world that probably came right out of a Boy Scout manual. But after a few years...' He looked at her and through her, seeing something that she knew had meaning only to himself. '...after a few years, I knew I'd had it with taking senseless orders from stupid leaders. So I quit.'

Blair smiled. 'Not James Bond,' she said softly. 'Don Quixote.'

Hunter laughed. 'And just as anachronistic. There I was, twenty-seven years old, with no skills the world seemed the least bit interested in. I tried a semester at university but...' He shrugged expressively. 'It was too far removed from reality. So I took a hard look at myself, figured out what I was good at, got in touch with some people I'd met while I worked for the Company...'

'...and here you are, in a farmhouse in Tuscany...'

'Here I am, in *my* farmhouse in Tuscany...'

'Is it really yours?'

He nodded. 'I bought it three years ago. I was in Florence, on business. It was a spur of the moment kind of thing.'

'I don't blame you for falling in love with it,' Blair said. 'The house, the hills, the isolation...'

'You're right, but it was nothing that romantic. In my line of work, it pays to have places where you can go to ground in an emergency.'

'What they call a safe house?' She laughed at the look of surprise on his face. 'More James Bond, I'm afraid.'

Hunter grinned. 'But accurate. Actually, I thought about selling the place just a few months ago. But I'm glad I didn't. If I had, I wouldn't be here, boring a beautiful woman to death...'

'Me?' Her voice was a whisper.

'I don't see anyone else in the room, do you?' He looked into her eyes and smiled. 'You're an enigma, Meryl Blair Desmond,' he said softly. 'Sometimes you seem so damned innocent and... Are you sure you're the same woman who announced she wanted to go down in the Guinness Book of Records as having danced in every fountain in every capital city in the world?'

Blair blinked. 'Did I... is that what I said?'

Rhys laughed. 'That's a quote straight out of your file.' He took a step towards her. 'But you're not anything like that woman, Blair.'

Her eyes closed, and then opened slowly as he reached out and touched her cheek.

'All that proves,' she said breathlessly, 'is that sometimes things aren't the way they seem to be. Everything isn't always black or white...'

Behind them, the pot hissed suddenly as hot liquid bubbled over its sides and spilled on to the fire. Rhys grabbed the handle and shoved it to the back of the stove. He sniffed appreciatively.

'OK,' he said solemnly, 'you're right.'

Blair looked at him in surprise. 'I am?'

He laughed as he ruffled her hair. 'Things aren't always black or white, at least, not when it comes to food. Ratatouille may sound like hell, but it smells like heaven.'

CHAPTER NINE

BLAIR stirred as the voices of Simon and Garfunkel faded into the silence of the car. Beside her, Hunter glanced away from the road just long enough to remove the tape from the cassette player and insert another. She smiled as she recognised the Debussy melody, its soft poignancy a perfect match for the rainy greyness of the day.

'I like your taste in music, Hunter.'

Hunter grinned. 'I was just thinking the same thing about you, Miss Desmond.' He glanced at her as she smothered a yawn. 'Tired?'

'Umm——' she said, arching her back. 'A little.' An embarrassed smile tugged at the corners of her mouth. 'Although I can't imagine why. I don't think I've ever slept twelve hours straight before.'

He laughed softly. 'All on one glass of wine. You should have told me the effect alcohol has on you right at the start. I'd have waved an open bottle of wine under your nose that first day and I wouldn't have had a minute's trouble with you after that.'

Blair smiled as she lay her head back against the seat, watching as the wipers moved slowly across the windscreen.

'Aunt Annie would have called me a cheap drunk.'

'I'm beginning to think I'd like to meet this aunt of yours,' Hunter said. 'She sounds like a lady after my own heart.'

'You'd like her,' Blair said, before she could stop herself. 'And she'd like you.'

Hunter reached across the console and clasped her hand lightly in his. 'I guess you take after her side of the family, hmm?'

Satisfied, Blair? 'Something like that,' she said carefully.

'Where does she live?'

'In . . . in the States.'

His eyebrows rose. 'How many chances do I get to guess which one?'

She laughed, wondering if the laugh sounded as forced as it felt. 'Come on, Hunter. Stop playing private eye. What is this, a security check?'

He glanced at her and then back at the road. 'It's what's known as getting to know someone better. Do you realise I've talked my fool head off, and I still don't know anything about you?'

'You know everything about me,' she said. Her voice sounded stilted, even to her own ears, and she forced a smile to her lips. 'I mean, you've got everything about me filed away in a drawer, haven't you? What more could you possibly want to know?'

Hunter shrugged his shoulders. 'The information that makes up a client profile is usually pretty superficial.' He glanced at her and smiled. 'Although what I recall of yours is rather intriguing.'

Jealousy shot through her so suddenly and sharply that it hurt. Stop that! she told herself. Are you crazy? He thinks you're Meryl, doesn't he? You can't be jealous of that . . .

'Meaning?' she asked carefully.

He smiled. 'It said you danced in fountains. But it didn't say you know all the words to "Mrs Robinson". Or that you can make a mean ratatouille. Or that you cry when you hear gypsy violins . . .'

Blair laughed softly. 'I wasn't crying, I was laughing. I've never heard such strange stuff over the radio. What did' you say that was? A Yugoslavian programme?'

He nodded. 'I'm glad I remembered that old portable radio was in the cupboard.' He glanced at her, and then back at the road. 'Did you really enjoy last night?'

'Of course I did,' she said, smiling at him. 'Well, I did until that second glass of Chianti hit...'

'Are you sure?'

The laughter had left his voice. 'Yes,' she said softly. His hand covered hers. 'I'm glad,' he said simply.

A heavy silence filled the car, and finally Blair cleared her throat. 'Did you? Enjoy last night, I mean?'

He glanced at her and a teasing smile lit his face. 'It was terrific—right up until the second you passed out.'

Blair winced. 'I can't believe I did that. I'm just glad... I thought drunks babbled on endlessly. Are you sure I didn't?'

'God, woman, you've asked me that half a dozen times,' he said with a groan. 'What dark secrets do you have? I told you, you were fine. There we were, waltzing around the kitchen, and suddenly you got this strange look on your face...'

'No more wine for me,' she said with conviction.

Hunter nodded. 'I agree,' he said solemnly. 'It's bad for a man's reputation to carry a woman to bed, tuck her in, and spend the rest of the night sleeping on the floor, listening to her snore.'

Blair laughed. 'I don't snore. And if you don't mind sleeping on the floor, why didn't you the other night?'

He shrugged. 'The circumstances were different, remember?'

Yes, she thought, laying her head back against the seat, they certainly were. A few days ago, the man beside her had terrified her. Now, the same man could bring a smile to her face with just a word. He could make her feel more contentment than she'd ever known just by coming into the room. He could make her heart turn over when he touched her, even if it were only to take her hand in his. And when he kissed her—oh, God, when he kissed her...

A tremor rippled through her as she remembered the taste and feel of his mouth. The intensity of her feelings frightened her. She had read of passion, seen it depicted on the screen, but nothing had prepared her for the fire that swept through her when she was in Rhys's arms. She wanted him to caress her, to whisper things no man had whispered before—even though the still rational part of her mind told her that was not only impossible, it was dangerous.

It was getting harder and harder to remember that she was playing a role. And yet, that was the only reason she was here, riding along a dusty road beside this man she hadn't even known existed three days ago. If she hadn't agreed to do Meryl a favour... if everything had gone smoothly at the airport... if she hadn't at first thought lying would save her life... Never mind all that, Blair. The simple truth is that you're here, pretending to be someone you're not, lying to a man who believes in you...

She shifted uncomfortably. Drinking that Chianti last night had been incredibly foolish. She never drank anything more than a bit of sherry—how many times had Meryl teased her about that? Well, she hadn't been thinking straight. They'd been having such a good time, laughing and talking and...

She glanced over at him. Was it possible she'd wanted to get drunk? She was too much a coward to tell him the truth sober, but if the wine had loosened her tongue... No, she thought, looking away from him, no, that was too crazy. It was simply that they'd been having so much fun last night. Rhys had produced a bouquet

of wild flowers for the centre of the table, and then he'd
lit candles to dine by. And then, after dinner, he'd remembered that old radio.

'It won't work,' he'd said, fiddling with the dial. 'The
batteries are years old.'

But it *had* worked. They'd picked up some tinny
station playing sad gypsy music.

'Ahh, Natasha, may I have this dance?' Rhys had
asked.

And she'd curtsied and settled into his arms, and he'd
whirled her around the room, faster and faster, until
suddenly everything had begun to spin wildly and...

When she awakened, she was alone. The bed felt chill
and damp; she could hear rain pattering lightly on the
tile roof, the sound of the drops like tiny explosions in
her head. And when she sat up, her stomach seemed to
rise with her. She pushed the blanket aside and swung
her feet to the floor. She was in her underthings—the
spare set from Meryl's carry-on—although she couldn't
remember having got undressed. But there were her
trousers and her sweater, neatly folded and lying on the
dresser. But how...?

'Rhys,' she whispered, closing her eyes, recalling the
shadowy memory of strong arms lifting her and putting
her gently on the bed and firm, warm lips against hers
and...

'Coffee will make you feel better.' Hunter grinned
from the doorway. 'Come on,' he said, holding out a
mug. 'You can do it.'

Well, she thought, pulling up the blanket and clutching
it to her, he was still talking to her. And he was smiling,
all of which meant she hadn't let anything slip last night.
It did mean that, didn't it?

'I'm not sure I can do anything,' she mumbled. 'What
happened to me?'

He laughed aloud. 'You passed out in the middle of dinner, that's what happened. You looked at your second glass of *vino* and wham, that was it.'

'Wham?' she repeated, touching her hand lightly to her aching head.

'It was as if somebody had hit you with a good right cross to the chin,' he said. 'One minute you were perfectly fine, and the next you were in never-never land.' He grinned and waggled the mug at her. 'Come on, drink this down and you'll feel better.'

She tossed the blanket over her shoulder and got to her feet. She felt better already, knowing she hadn't said anything she shouldn't—at least, until she started padding across the room. Then her stomach began to complain.

'I... I'm not sure I can get that coffee down,' she said doubtfully.

'Just drink,' Rhys urged, holding the mug to her lips. 'Take it all in one big swallow.'

Blair wrinkled her nose. 'Ugh—what is that stuff? It doesn't smell like coff...'

She gagged as he tilted the mug to her mouth. Whatever he was feeding her was vile. She tried to turn away, but his other hand caught the back of her head and held her still.

'Drink it,' he commanded. 'If you make me spoon-feed it to you, it'll only take longer and taste worse.'

She knew better than to doubt him. His voice told her he meant every word, and Aunt Annie had once doused her with castor oil in much the same way. Blair closed her eyes and swallowed.

'That's it. A little more. Good girl,' he said, beaming at her. 'Now, that wasn't so awful, was it?'

She shuddered. 'You said you had coffee in that mug,' she said accusingly.

He laughed and tweaked her nose. 'I said coffee would make you feel better. And it will, now that you've had a dose of Mandrake the Medic's Magic Elixir.'

'Mandrake the Medic's what?' she asked, laughing in spite of herself.

'Magic Elixir.' He grinned at her over his shoulder as he walked into the kitchen. 'It's what the medic in my platoon used to feed the guys for a hangover.'

'I haven't got a hangover,' Blair said indignantly, padding after him. 'I just feel a little under the weather.'

Hunter grinned and handed her a mug. 'Coffee,' he said. 'Honest.'

She peered at him doubtfully, but there was no mistaking the aroma of the dark, steaming liquid.

'All right,' she said with a sigh, 'I believe you.' The blanket slipped off her shoulder as she reached for the mug and she tugged it up quickly. 'Er—by the way, Hunter, thank you for...' A wash of rose tinged her cheeks. 'I assume you put me to bed,' she said at last, forcing her eyes to remain on his.

'I did,' he said politely. 'It was purely in the line of duty, of course.'

Blair nodded. 'Of course,' she said with dignity. 'Thank you.'

'You're welcome.'

There was laughter in his grey eyes, but she refused to acknowledge it. Besides, it was silly to feel embarrassed, wasn't it? This was the same man who had forcibly undressed her two nights ago. He'd seen her in her underclothes before. But it was different now. Everything was different...

Hunter reached out and touched his hand to her cheek. 'I was an absolute gentleman,' he said softly.

The colour in her cheeks darkened. 'I'm sure you were. I...'

'I want you wide awake when I make love to you, Blair.'

His voice was husky, his words a whisper. Her eyes widened in surprise as they met the silver heat of his. *When,* he'd said, not *if...* The breath caught in her throat. His hand was still against her cheek, the touch of his fingers suddenly electric.

'Rhys,' she whispered and then she swallowed, searching for something to say, but he smiled and touched his fingers to her mouth.

'We've got to drive into Florence,' he said. 'I wish to hell we didn't, but I don't want to take any chances. Being stuck out here with the car the way it is could be bad news.'

'Yes,' she said gratefully, letting her breath out, 'the car...'

'The trip's going to take longer than it should. I don't want to put too much strain on the car.'

She nodded. 'Right. Just let me get dressed...'

He smiled. 'Drink your coffee first. I made it strong and sweet.'

'But I never take sugar.'

'Drink,' he said firmly. 'Go on.'

She sighed as she lifted the mug to her lips. 'Doesn't anyone ever win an argument with you, Hunter?' His only answer was a smile, and she sighed again and then gulped the coffee down. 'Satisfied?'

'No,' he said, 'not quite.'

'But I drank the coffee. Every drop.'

'You haven't said good morning to me.'

'Of course I have. I...' The look in his eyes was unyielding and she blew out her breath. 'All right. Good morning.'

He shook his head. 'Try it again.'

'Hunter, I...'

'Rhys,' he said softly.

She felt a rush of heat as she looked at him. It was such a simple request—or was it? She felt as if he were asking her something more, something she was afraid to answer...

And then he smiled into her eyes and she was lost. 'Good morning, Rhys,' she whispered.

His hand went to the nape of her neck and she swayed towards him, but all he did was kiss her lightly on the tip of her nose.

'Good morning, Blair,' he murmured. 'Isn't that a better way to start the day?'

And it was. By the time they were ready to leave the farmhouse, the rain had abated. Her headache had vanished, as had her queasy stomach. She'd dressed in the same trousers and sweater she'd worn the day before—it was too chilly to wear the cotton skirt and blouse she'd bought at the market in Fiorello. She'd tossed her jacket over her shoulders and fluffed her hair away from her face, peering at herself in the age-rimed mirror that hung in the bedroom.

'Stop fussing,' Hunter had said, giving her an unceremonious slap on the bottom as he went by. 'You look terrific.'

But she didn't, she thought now, stealing a glance at him as they wound down the narrow road that led to Florence. Her clothing was rumpled, the rain had spun her hair into a soft halo of curls, and the light had been so bad she hadn't risked any make-up but lipstick. She probably looked the way she'd looked when she and Aunt Annie got off the bus from Iowa four years ago, six months after Uncle Edgar had closed his eyes for ever.

Aunt Annie had sold the farm the week Blair had graduated from high school. 'I'm too old for another Iowa winter,' she'd said in answer to Blair's stunned questions. 'We're moving to San Diego, where the sun shines all the time. My cousin Helen lives in a retirement community, and she says it's wonderful there.'

It had been—for Aunt Annie. Blair had waited until her aunt was settled in, and then she'd announced that she was going to live in Los Angeles.

'But I'll come home weekends,' she'd promised.

It had been easy to find a job in LA, and only a little harder to locate a tiny apartment. And she'd made a couple of friends—no special ones, though. People didn't seem to settle in the city long enough for that. She dated a few men, although none of them were special, either. And then, without warning, the firm she worked for had gone under and Blair was out of work. And then fate stepped in, fate and a rather cryptic ad in the employment section of the Sunday paper.

'Companion/Secretary,' the ad read. 'Exciting opportunity.'

It had been too appealing to pass up. Blair had written for an interview—and she'd met Meryl.

'Are you really from Iowa?' Meryl had teased. 'I didn't know anybody lived way out in the middle of the map.'

Of course, Meryl had teased her about everything. The way she dressed, the way she wore her hair. The way she used make-up.

'This is Los Angeles,' Meryl had laughed. 'Pretty girls are a dime a dozen. Why look pretty when you can look beautiful?' And when Blair had protested, Meryl had teased her all the more.

'And there's no need to get all blushy and gushy, Miss Prim and Proper. Don't tell me the boys back home never told you you were pretty!'

Blair risked a quick look at Hunter again. Yes, she thought, some of them had told her that. But it was different, hearing it from someone like him. It had never occurred to her before that just looking at someone—at a man—could be so pleasurable. And it wasn't just the way he looked. It was...it was everything about him. The way he moved, the way he sounded, the way he commanded a room just by his presence.

Did other women feel that way about him? Yes, she thought, of course they did. There were probably lots of women in his life, women far more experienced and interesting than she. Suddenly, she hated them all, hated those unknown women who had known what it felt like to be held in those strong arms, kissed by those warm lips, touched by those hard hands...

Hunter's hand closed over hers. 'Are you awake?' She nodded, and his fingers tightened their grip. 'Then look out your window.'

Blair turned her head and drew in her breath. 'Florence?' she asked, looking into the valley below. 'Oh, Rhys, it's beautiful!'

The city was a jumble of red tile roofs clustered on a valley floor which stretched towards softly rolling green hills beyond. A shimmer of water lay in the far distance—the River Arno, Blair thought with a shiver of excitement.

Rhys smiled at her. 'Even the rain's on our side. The tourists will all be indoors in the museums, hiding from the weather.'

'I don't mind the rain,' she assured him. 'I want to see everything. Can we do that?'

He chuckled softly. 'Absolutely. We'll buy ourselves the biggest umbrella we can find, and I'll show you Florence. The *piazzas* and the bridges and a little church that has a fresco tucked away in a corner that has to be a Caravaggio and...' He glanced at Blair and shook his head. 'You've really never been here before?'

She took a deep breath. 'I told you I haven't. Why, did it say something different than that in my file?'

Rhys grinned. 'I just can't believe you never saw Florence, that's all. Some people think it's as beautiful as Paris or Venice...'

Her heart hammered. 'Really? I never heard that before.'

He shrugged his shoulders. 'Actually, I've never been to Venice, so I wouldn't know.' Thank God for that, she thought. 'And as for Paris, well, everybody loves Paris.'

'Right,' she said casually. 'But...isn't Florence a much smaller city?'

She felt weak with relief when he rose to the bait and began to talk about the city, pointing out landmarks as they entered its rain-slicked streets, narrow and shadowed like part of some huge labyrinth. But he seemed to know exactly where he was going. Within minutes, they pulled up before a closed garage door.

'I'll just be a minute,' he said, slamming the car door behind him.

He vanished inside the building. When he reappeared, he was laughing and talking with a muscular, fair-haired man dressed in spotless overalls. The man inclined his head in Blair's direction and she smiled in return.

'Carlo's just going to take a look,' Hunter called, and she nodded.

Carlo knelt beside the car and peered beneath it, then straightened up and leaned on the fender, rocking the car gently from side to side, all the while tilting his head as if he were listening to his patient's heartbeat. Finally, he turned to Hunter and shook his head, a look of obvious sympathy on his face.

'Yes, you're right. There is a problem, Hunter. Bring it inside,' he said in clear but heavily accented English.

The garage door rose slowly, revealing a cluttered interior. Hunter drove the Lamborghini on to a ramp, sighing as he shut off the ignition.

'Well, I'm not really surprised... Carlo thinks it's probably the ball joints, but he won't know until he gets her up on the lift.'

'You look upset,' Blair said softly. 'Are you afraid it's something more serious than that?'

Hunter laughed and shook his head. 'I'm not worried about the car, Blair. I asked Carlo if he knew a rental agency where I could get my hands on a Rover or something similar.'

'And?'

'And, unfortunately, he doesn't.'

'Why not?'

He ran his fingers through his hair. 'You can't get a vehicle that specialised without putting in an order ahead of time, and we can't afford to wait around. If something comes down, I'd rather we were at the farmhouse. There's a clear field of view in all directions—it's an easier defence when there's only one man.'

Blair looked at him and shook her head. 'What are you talking about, Rhys?'

He sighed as he got out of the car and slammed the door behind him. 'Blair,' he said softly as he opened her door, 'I don't want to upset you, but we can't afford to take risks. As far as I know, no one's after us. I'll telephone Rome later and make certain, but... Blair, sweetheart, what is it?'

If only she could tell him, she thought. If only she had the courage to say, Rhys, it's all been a terrible mistake. Desmond sent you on a wild-goose chase... But the deception wasn't only Oscar Desmond's. It was hers, too. And the guilt that had troubled her yesterday was changing somehow. What she felt now was more than guilt. It was... it was...

Rhys put his finger beneath her chin and lifted her face to his. 'Don't be frightened, Blair,' he said softly. 'I'll take care of you.' He smiled into her eyes. 'Now stop looking like that, or Carlo will think you're not happy with me and he won't keep his promise.'

She forced herself to return his smile. 'What promise?'

'He's going to make some phone calls and try and find something for us.' Rhys grinned. 'For you, actually, for *la bella signorina*—and believe me, if anyone can do it, he can. He knows every decent car within a hundred miles of here. And I trust him.'

Rhys was right. Carlo made three calls. The last was lengthy and, even though Blair couldn't understand a word of it, she suspected he was alternately cajoling, bullying, and finally promising the moon to whomever was at the other end. When he hung up the phone, he was smiling.

'*Fantastico,* Hunter. The cousin of a cousin of my wife has what you need.'

An hour later, they were bounding along the cobblestoned streets in a vehicle that looked like a Land Rover but sounded like a race car. Carlo had tinkered with the engine for a few minutes and then smiled modestly.

'I made some minor adjustments, Hunter,' he'd said, handing over the keys. 'I think you'll be pleased.'

By the time Rhys had gunned the purring engine and taken the Rover through its paces in the twisting, narrow streets, he was more than pleased.

'Terrific,' he said happily. 'This baby will eat up those mountain roads and come back for more. Now we can play at being tourists for a while. How does that sound?'

Blair smiled. 'It sounds wonderful.'

Their first stop was at an elegant leather shop. It was the sort of place Meryl Desmond probably frequented, but it brought Blair up short.

'We can't go in there,' she said, pulling back as Rhys started to open the door. 'We look like wrecks.'

'For shame, Meryl Blair Desmond,' he said softly, tugging her into the store after him. 'You should know better. Just act as if you expected to be treated like visiting royalty. Watch.'

She learned, to her absolute delight, that he was right. The handsomely dressed clerk looked visibly distressed at the sight of these two rumpled, damp individuals, but Hunter persisted in being the very soul of courtesy and charm. He acted as if the shop and its personnel had been placed on the Via Tournabuoni for his consideration. By the time he took out his credit card to pay for his purchases, the clerk was all smiles and gushes.

'Rhys, this will cost you a fortune,' Blair whispered as he helped her into a buttery-soft leather jacket.

'It's wet and cold out there, Blair. You need something to wear if we're going to walk along the Arno, see the Piazza della Signoria, stand in line to see Michelangelo's David and still stay dry enough to have lunch at the best restaurant in Tuscany.' He smiled as he buttoned the jacket from top to bottom. 'Take a look in the mirror and see how you like it.'

But the touch of his fingers made her tremble, and when she sought her reflection, all she could see was Rhys, standing beside her.

'I...it looks lovely,' she said finally.

His eyes met hers.

'Yes,' he murmured, 'lovely.'

It rained steadily all day, the sky changing only from leaden grey to soggy charcoal as the hours waned. Rhys showed her his own Florence, and yet, through it all, Blair knew he was constantly on the alert. His arm felt like a protective shield wrapped around her. His eyes were never still, but always seemed to be looking past her into shadowed corners and up the narrow streets. He was cautious, even in the beautiful restaurant where they had lunch, politely requesting a table in a secluded corner, and then seating himself so that he had a clear view of the entrance door.

The rain stopped suddenly in late afternoon while they were walking through the Boboli Gardens, high above the heart of the city. Rhys looked up at the still-threatening sky and then furled the umbrella he'd bought.

'Thank God,' he laughed. 'I was beginning to be afraid we'd turn into toadstools.'

'On a beautiful day like this? Don't be silly.'

He slipped his arm around her waist. 'Beautiful? Have you been at the Chianti again, Miss Desmond?'

She wanted to tell him that it had been the most perfect day she'd ever spent because she'd spent it with him, but she only smiled.

'I've been at something I can't pronounce,' she said. 'What was that wine you ordered in the restaurant? Barlow something or other...'

Rhys grinned. 'A Barolo '64. A modest little offering, don't you think?'

'A man who orders a wine that's older than I am and *costata alla fiorentina* and *insalata* whatever it was, probably isn't a stranger to French cooking either, is he?'

Hunter's face was a study in innocence. 'Maybe not.'

'Which means he knows all about ratatouille...'

His lips twisted in a quick smile. 'He might.'

'Especially if he has an office in Paris... You do, don't you, Hunter?'

'Well,' he said, shrugging his shoulders, 'now that you ask, ma'am...'

Blair laughed up at him. 'If you utter one "golly" or "by gosh", I swear, I'll hit you, Rhys Hunter.'

Rhys drew her closer to him. 'I'm glad you had a good time today, Blair.' He smiled. 'You know, for a girl who has everything, you're amazingly easy to please.'

Her smile wavered. 'I keep telling you that you don't know the real me.'

'I guess I don't,' he teased. 'Anyone would have thought I'd bought you diamonds on the Ponte Vechhio this afternoon instead of *gelati*.'

She laughed softly. 'Well, I like ice-cream. It was my favourite dessert when I was a child.'

'I'll bet you were a cute little girl,' he said, taking her hand in his. 'What did you look like? Did you wear your hair in pigtails? Did you have braces on your teeth?'

'Yes and yes,' she laughed. 'Although my mother always said...' Her voice drifted off into silence. *Careful, Blair. Careful...*

'Go on,' Hunter prompted gently. 'What did she say?'

'She said the braces hadn't changed much of anything, that I still had an overbite...'

Rhys's arm went behind her and he drew her to him. 'Now that you mention it,' he said softly, 'I guess she was right. But I think it's sexy as hell. It makes you look as if you're waiting to be kissed.' He looked into her eyes and then at her mouth. 'Are you waiting, Blair?' he whispered. 'Do you want me to taste you again, to touch you...'

I want you to love me as I love you.

The unexpected words rang so clearly inside her that for a second Blair was certain she'd said them aloud. But she hadn't; Rhys was still looking at her through narrow, half-closed eyes, still waiting for her answer. Tears filled her eyes as the silken threads of her own deception began to close around her.

'Rhys,' she whispered, 'you...you don't understand...I'm not...I wasn't expecting...'

'Neither was I,' he said thickly, drawing her tightly against him. 'But why should we waste whatever time we have left? Before you know it, we'll be back in Rome. And then...'

Suddenly, his body stiffened against hers with a tension that turned her blood to ice. His encircling arms became bands of steel; she heard him mutter a short, one syllable word under his breath.

'Rhys?' she murmured, looking into his eyes. But they were focused beyond her, on something in the distance.

'Quiet,' he said.

'Rhys, what's the matter?' His face looked as if it had been carved from stone. No, she thought, remembering the statue of David, not even that. Stone, in the hands of Michelangelo, had more warmth than Hunter's face at this moment. 'Rhys,' she whispered, 'please, you're frightening me.'

'There's a bench behind you, Blair, in that alcove. When I let go of you, I want you to turn, walk to it, and sit down.'

'What is it? Is something . . .'

'Sit down and stay there, no matter what happens. Do you understand?'

'Yes,' she said, shivering in his embrace. 'But . . .' The protest died on her lips. She had never seen Rhys look this way before. His eyes were like grey stones, his nostrils flared. He took a step backwards and then another; she could see the coiled tension in his body, the knotted power waiting to be unleashed.

'Now!' His voice was like a whip, commanding her to do as he'd ordered.

Trembling, she turned towards the bench and sank down on it, but not before she'd seen the dark gleam of the gun in Rhys's hand.

CHAPTER TEN

BLAIR had never been more frightened in her life. Long after Rhys had vanished into the shadows, she could still remember the sight of his gun, metallic and deadly, as it lay in the palm of his hand. What had he seen? she wondered, wrapping her arms around herself as a rain-laden wind blew suddenly through the cypresses. But she knew what he'd seen. He'd seen someone—someone his instincts told him was a threat. That was the only reason he'd have looked so grim, sounded so...so cold, so frightening...

Where was he? The seconds ticked into minutes and still she sat alone, trying to see beyond the shadows. The sun would set soon and the shadows would lengthen until the gardens would be as black as a mine-shaft. Suppose he hadn't returned by then? What would she do?

She stood and took a few hesitant steps across the terrace. Hunter had disappeared into a stand of trees, but he could be anywhere by now. And anything could have happened to him. God only knew who had been lurking in the shadows. No one knew they were in the Tuscan Hills—no, she thought, that wasn't quite right. What no one knew was where Meryl Desmond was. Oh, it was so complicated. Why hadn't she told him the truth?

The rain had started again, this time with a wind-driven force that seemed to be driving straight through the leather jacket Rhys had bought her, chilling her to the marrow. The jacket was just one more way he'd tried to protect her, another knot in the skein of deceits that was wrapping around her. She'd let him go on believing

142

half-truths as if this were all some harmless game—but what had happened at the airport wasn't a game. Suppose they'd been followed from Rome? Anything was possible. For all she knew, Hunter was locked in deadly struggle with a killer out there in the darkness. He could be hurt. He could be...

No, please... Blair squeezed her eyes shut, but the image of Rhys, lying cold and still on the rain-soaked ground, remained vivid.

'Rhys,' she whispered. 'Rhys...'

'Blair?'

A sob burst from her throat at the sound of his voice behind her. She called out his name again, then turned blindly and threw herself into his arms. He held her tightly against him, his chin against the top of her head. She nestled against his chest, breathing his scent, listening to the rapid thud of his heart. She could hear the air rasping in and out of his lungs.

'Blair,' he whispered, his arms around her a refuge for her fear, 'it's all right, sweet, it's all right.'

'I was so scared,' she murmured. 'Oh, Rhys, I imagined...I thought...'

He rocked her gently, crooning softly to her. 'Shh,' he said, 'shh, everything is going to be fine.'

'Wh-what happened? Did you...was there someone out there?'

He let out his breath. 'Yes,' he said finally. 'A man.'

Blair's heart thudded erratically. 'Did you...did you catch him?'

He shook his head. 'No,' he said tightly.

'But...you were gone so long,' she whispered. 'I thought...I thought...I was afraid...'

His arms tightened around her. 'I was gone too damned long,' he said gruffly. 'It was stupid of me. I should never have left you alone.'

'I wasn't afraid for myself,' she said quickly. 'I was afraid for you. I thought something had happened to you.'

'Come on,' he said gruffly. 'Let's get the hell out of here. Can you make it down that slope? We'll get back to the car a lot faster than if we take the pathway.'

'But what happened, Rhys? Aren't you going to tell me?'

'Later,' he said flatly. 'When we're safe.'

A chill danced across her shoulders. 'Safe?' Her voice was a thready whisper and she cleared her throat. 'Is somebody after us?'

'Just hold on to my hand and watch your footing,' Rhys said. 'The grass is slippery.'

Suddenly, the garden seemed ominous. Shadows she knew were only trees seemed to reach out towards her; a nightbird called out once, its voice high and piercing, and she shivered. But Rhys's hand clasped her tightly. The strength and warmth of his body seemed to infuse a courage to hers as he led her down the grassy hill to the street where they'd left the Land Rover. It was only when they were finally locked safely inside it that she let out a shaky laugh.

'You scared the life out of me back there, Rhys.'

He glanced into the rear view mirror as he gunned the engine to life. 'I didn't mean to,' he said, pulling out from the kerb. 'I just didn't want to take any more chances than I already have.'

The Rover's headlights cut a narrow swath through the wet darkness. Rhys switched on the windscreen wipers; their soft sound seemed to fill the car.

'Chances? What chances.'

His eyes slid to the rear view mirror again. 'Where would you like to begin?' he asked grimly. 'For starters, I should never have left you alone on that terrace. If there was somebody following us...'

'If? You mean, you're not certain?'

He shook his head. 'I'm not, no. I saw somebody in the shadows. But I never caught up to him—I realised I'd left you alone. If there was somebody up there, if he had a partner...'

Blair shivered. 'Is there—does this car have a heater? I'm terribly cold.'

'You're soaked through,' he said, looking at her and then back at the road. 'There's a rug in the back seat, under some magazines—I saw it this morning. Can you reach it?'

Blair unbuckled her seat-belt and twisted around in the seat. 'Yes,' she said, 'I can just about...' Her teeth chattered as she wrapped the musty blanket around herself.

'Better?'

'Ye...hes.'

'Take a deep breath. And another. Good girl.' His voice softened and his hand covered hers. 'Don't be frightened, Blair. I won't let anything happen to you.'

Guilt cut through her. 'I know you won't,' she whispered, running her tongue across her dry lips. 'Rhys? That man in the park—there are lots of reasons he might have been standing there.'

Rhys nodded. 'Absolutely.'

'Then why—why did you react that way?'

His eyes were glued to the mirror. Blair turned her head and looked out the rear window. A car was overtaking them; its headlights grew larger and larger, until finally it pulled abreast of the Rover and passed them. She let out her breath as it pulled away.

'Why did I react what way?'

She turned her head and looked at him. 'You jumped to the worst possible conclusion the second you saw that man.'

He shrugged his shoulders. 'It's one of the things you learn in this business. Yeah, there were a dozen reasons to explain why a guy would stand in the shadows on a rainy night. He might have been walking his dog. Maybe he'd had a fight with his wife and wanted to cool off.' He laughed unpleasantly. 'Hell, for all I know, he was a peeper. Maybe he gets his kicks watching couples make love.'

'Then, if you thought of all those things, why...'

'Because he could have been there for another reason, one that would have endangered you. And it wasn't worth taking the chance.'

'And...and the gun?'

'The first thing you learn about guns is the most important.' He looked across the car at her and then back at the road. 'Never carry one unless you're prepared to use it.'

Her throat felt as if it were closing. 'And you'd use it to protect Meryl Desmond?'

'Don't tell me we're going to have a debate about gun control.'

She managed a small, shaky laugh. 'It's just a simple question, Rhys.'

'Hell, guns kill. That's the only function they have— no one wants to use a gun.'

She looked at him and then at the rain-swept road. 'But you'd use it if you had to.'

He looked at her; in the faint light from the dashboard, she could see the frown on his face.

'What's going on, Blair?'

'It's just that—there's a risk, isn't there? I mean, suppose...suppose you were protecting somebody and...and you made a mistake.'

'No one's infallible,' he said quietly. 'We all make mistakes.'

'But that kind of mistake...the kind we're talking about...' Blair's voice dropped to a whisper. 'That's a terrible responsibility, isn't it?'

Rhys nodded. 'Yes, it is,' he said flatly. 'When I worked for the Company...' His voice hardened. 'Maybe it's different now...but in those days, they used the men in the field like chess pieces. They sat in their offices, playing their games, a million miles removed from the real world. And they manipulated us. Hell, we were expendable. All that mattered was the game.' She heard the breath rasp in his throat and then his hand sought hers. 'Do you understand what I'm saying, Blair? There are bastards out there who think this is a game, but I never have.'

Weeks later, Blair would remember that moment as if it had been frozen in time. She would remember the sound of the windscreen wipers, the patter of the rain, the rawness in Rhys's voice—but most of all she would remember the swelling sorrow that rose within her, like a giant hand closing around her throat and keeping the air from her lungs. She could barely breathe, and she knew she couldn't speak, and so she simply nodded and returned the pressure of Rhys's fingers while she stared blindly ahead into the blackness of the rain-chilled night.

The lie she'd been living the past days had become hard to bear, but now it was agony. How could she have been so stupid? Everything Rhys had done, from that moment at the airport, had been for her safety. But tonight—tonight, for the first time, she had finally realised that the rules of his profession could be deadly. This wasn't the simple charade Meryl and her father had asked her to perform. Rhys would be angry when he knew the truth, Oscar Desmond had said. She could still hear that self-confident whisper.

'I'll straighten things out,' he'd assured her, but she knew with a piercing clarity that he'd never be able to do that. Game players never saw the pieces bleed.

She thought of the man in the shadows, the gun in Rhys's hand, and she shuddered. What if Rhys had caught him? Someone might have been killed. Dear God, she thought, turning her face to the window. She wanted to curse, to pound her fist against the dashboard. Damn both the Desmonds! 'It's just a harmless gag,' Meryl had said, but there was nothing harmless about what she'd been doing. She was playing a terrible game, a dangerous game.

That was what Rhys had tried to tell her at the beginning, when he'd thought she was making light of all his efforts to keep her safe. How he'd disliked her then— and how he'd despise her now, when he realised she'd used him, manipulated him in a game with no meaning.

She turned towards him quickly, before she lost her courage. 'Rhys,' she said, 'Rhys, listen...'

He gave her a quick smile. 'I thought you were asleep.'

'No, I...I wasn't asleep. I was thinking.' *Tell him!* 'Rhys...'

His hand closed over hers. 'You're still cold,' he said. 'We'll be at the farmhouse soon; I'll build us a fire. How does that sound?'

'Rhys, please, I...I...' She swallowed and drew in her breath. 'We...we never telephoned Rome today, did we?'

'Your father, you mean? We'll drive to Fiorello in the morning.' He cleared his throat. 'You must be eager to get back to Rome. This isn't the vacation you'd planned, is it?'

Her heart was beating wildly. 'Rhys, I have to tell you...

This vacation... It's not...' Her courage failed her and she began again. 'I have to tell you about me... about Meryl...'

'Later.'

She shook her head. 'No,' she said desperately, 'no, I can't put it off any longer. I should have told you days ago. I...'

'Dammit, Blair—later!'

His voice had turned hard and threatening, just as it had been earlier in the Boboli Gardens. Blair turned to him in surprise just as he reached out and killed the headlights. The black night seemed to close down around them.

'What is it?' she whispered. Her eyes flew to the rear view mirror. Had he been right? Was someone following them? 'Did you see something?'

The Rover slowed and stopped. 'Easy,' Rhys breathed. She felt him shift in the seat beside her. 'Where the hell... there it is,' he said.

Her pulse was galloping. 'What?' she asked, her voice barely audible. 'Not... not a gun...'

'No,' he said. 'The starlight scope—I just want to take a look at the house and...' She watched as he raised the scope and scanned the hill slowly. 'OK,' he said finally. 'Everything's looking good.'

'You did see something,' Blair insisted. 'Please, tell me the truth.'

The Rover was inching forward again. 'I am telling you the truth,' he said softly. 'This is just a precaution. There hasn't been another car behind us for better than half an hour. But I'd rather be safe than sorry. If we run without lights, we'll be damned near invisible on a night like this.' He touched her hand lightly. 'I just don't want to take any more chances.'

'I don't remember you taking any.'

'I took chances all day,' he said. A flint-edged grimness crept into his voice. 'What we did was crazy. We should have dropped off the Lamborghini, picked up the Rover, and got the hell out of Florence.'

A bittersweet sorrow filled her, and she spoke before she had time to consider her words. 'I'm glad we had today,' she murmured.

He laughed softly and laced his fingers through hers. 'So am I. It's been a terrific day—I just want to make sure it stays that way. Keep very still, and we'll do the last hundred yards with our eyes and ears open, OK?'

She held her breath while they drove towards the house. The rain had stopped, but the moon remained hidden behind a high bank of scudding clouds. The blackness outside the car had an almost palpable presence, the silence an ominous weight that seemed ready to crush her eardrums with its intensity. When Rhys turned off the engine, the silence became an oppressive entity.

'OK,' he said softly, 'I'm going to go in and check the house. You wait out here until I come for you.'

The thought of being separated from him terrified her. 'No,' she said quickly, 'I want to be with you.'

'Blair...'

She drew in her breath. 'Please.'

She heard him sigh. 'All right. Just stay behind me.'

As if she'd dare stay anywhere else, she thought, following after him. The door squeaked when he unlocked it and pushed it open; Rhys stepped into the room and she followed him as closely as his shadow. A single, narrow beam of light danced through the kitchen from the flashlight in his hand.

'Stay here,' he said after a moment.

'Rhys...'

'Stay here,' he repeated in a voice that permitted no argument.

Blair nodded, even though she knew he couldn't see her. She took a hesitant step back, then another, until finally she felt the cold press of the stone wall against her shoulders. Her eyes widened, trying to see into the blackness, but it was impossible. Where was Rhys? She couldn't hear a thing, not even the faintest footfall. God, where was he?

What was that? A rustling noise. Yes, there it was again. It was coming from the bedroom. No, from the passage beyond the bedroom. The outhouse, she thought suddenly. Had Rhys remembered to check the outhouse? Maybe she should go after him. Maybe...

Again! The rustling noise and a thump and, lord, please, no, no...

'Don't,' she cried as someone loomed out of the shadows, 'don't...'

Rhys's arms closed tightly around her. 'Blair, sweet, it's me. It's me.'

'Rhys.' His name was all she could think to say, all she was capable of. 'Rhys,' she said again, pressing her trembling body against his. 'I heard...I thought there was somebody...'

'Something, not somebody,' he chuckled. 'There was a mouse convention in the outhouse.'

Blair laughed softly, and the salty taste of her own tears filled her mouth.

'Thank God,' she whispered. 'You wouldn't believe the things I pictured...I'm sorry.'

Rhys shifted his body, settling her more closely against him. 'For what? Hell, never apologise for being frightened, Blair. We're all afraid sometimes.'

Suddenly, she became aware of the way he was holding her against him. The hard length of his body was pressed against hers from shoulder to thigh. Her cheek lay against his chest; beneath her ear, his heartbeat was strong and rapid. Her lashes fluttered closed as she drew in her breath. The smell of him filled her nostrils. All she had to do, she thought suddenly, was lift her hand and touch his face. His skin would be warm and supple beneath her fingers, and his mouth—his mouth...

'Don't you...don't you want to light the lamp?'

His hand cupped her head and lifted her face towards him. 'We don't need it,' he said softly. 'See? The moon is rising. I can see your cheek.' He bent his head and brushed his lips across her skin. 'And your eyes.' His lips moved gently across her closed eyelids. 'And your mouth.' She drew in her breath as his lips touched hers. 'I love the taste of your mouth,' he whispered as he kissed her. 'It tastes like honey. And cream. And...'

'Rhys, we can't...'

'We can. We can do whatever we want to do, whatever feels right. And this is right.' His lips touched her throat and her head fell back. 'You know it is. You've known it all along.' His fingers traced the outline of her lips. 'Tell me you want me,' he murmured. 'Tell me...'

His voice was husky, thick with a longing and a promise that made the blood begin to pound in her ears. And his mouth—oh, the feel of his mouth on her skin, on her earlobe, on her lips, the heated, firm caress of it, the taste of it...

'Please,' she said desperately. 'Rhys—you have to listen to me. I have to...I have to...'

'What are you afraid of? Is it me? Tell me it isn't.'

'No, no, not you,' she said, putting her hands against his chest. 'I'm not afraid of you, Rhys. Never of you.'

'We're safe here,' he whispered, catching her hand in his and lifting it to his lips. 'Trust me,' he breathed against her palm. 'Trust me, Blair. I'll never let anything hurt you.'

She moaned as he drew her fingers into his mouth, one at a time. 'Please,' she whispered, 'please, don't, don't...'

He bent his head to hers and kissed her. Her mouth parted as his lips touched hers, and she moaned again. His hands slipped beneath her jacket, beneath her sweater. They were hot and hard against her skin, and yet they felt like silk as they moved over her, touching her, gentling her.

'Rhys,' she gasped, twisting away from his seeking mouth, 'you have to listen to me. You don't know me. I'm not the woman you think I am...I...'

'Look at me,' he demanded. Slowly, she turned her face up to his. A watery moon had risen in the black sky, casting a strange half-light on his features. In the milky illumination, his eyes gleamed with silver flame as they looked into hers. 'Now tell me you don't want this,' he said thickly. She gasped as his hand cupped her breast over her thin cotton camisole. 'Tell me, and I'll stop.'

'I...I...' Her head fell back on her neck. She could feel her nipple press into his palm, feel her body arching towards his, seeking him as a flower seeks the sun. 'Rhys, please...'

'Please, what?' he whispered. 'Tell me, Blair. All you have to do is tell me what you want.'

His voice was rough, hard with demand and knowledge. And his eyes, those silvery eyes that seemed to burn her flesh, his eyes were telling her things, offering her things, secrets she had never known, never wanted to know, until now. Until Rhys. Her hands moved up his shirt and flattened against his chest. His heart raced beneath her palms, its beat as erratic and out of control as her own.

Tell him no, she thought desperately. Tell him he has to stop! Tell him that you've lied, that you've used him. Tell him, tell him...

But when she spoke, she could say only his name, over and over, in a whisper that told him everything he needed to know. A fierce smile of exultation swept across his face.

'I love to hear you say my name, do you know that?' he whispered. 'And I love to touch you, to kiss you...'

His mouth came down on hers, and desire flamed within her as his lips urged hers apart. She felt the thrust of his tongue in her mouth; the taste of him excited her, and she grasped his shirt, raising herself on tiptoe, her hips pressing against his in unconscious need. A sound came from the back of his throat and his body moved against hers.

'Tell me you want me as much as I want you,' he whispered.

Her arms snaked around his neck, and she drew his head down to hers. 'Kiss me,' she sighed in answer. 'Kiss me, Rhys. Don't stop. Don't...'

The breath caught in her throat as he crushed her to him, his mouth claiming hers in a kiss that made her knees tremble with weakness. He swung her into his arms, and she clung to him as he carried her through the silent house and into the bedroom. The scudding clouds above had turned the white moonlight shining through the window into a dizzying series of random flashes that illuminated the stark room with almost dreamworld intensity.

He lowered her to the bed gently, his lips still on hers, and a quicksilver excitement began to spread through her, flaming to life within her mind as well as her body, bathing her in a flood of sweet fire so achingly intense that she felt her bones melting. Rhys whispered her name against her mouth, and she sighed his. And then her clothing was falling away from her until the damp, jasmine-scented night air danced on her skin.

His fingers were licks of flame on her ribs, on her breast, and, when he bent his head and caught her nipple in his mouth, she cried out at the sensation. She clasped the back of his head, digging her hands into the thick, silky hair at the nape of his neck, feeling as if he were drawing the very soul from her body with the urgency of his kisses.

Her eyes flew open as he moved away from her. 'Rhys?'

'Yes,' he whispered, 'I'm just...'

She watched as he pulled his shirt over his head and tossed it aside, and then he got to his feet and pulled off his trousers. She'd been right, she thought, he *was* beautiful. Her gaze swept over his body unashamedly and then she raised her eyes to his face.

'Rhys,' she said, 'I've never... I haven't...'

Something flashed across his face—surprise, pleasure—it was too quick to be certain, and then he was beside her again, taking her in his arms, his skin hot against hers. He whispered her name as he tangled his fingers in her hair and brought her mouth to his.

'I'm glad,' he murmured.

She wanted to tell him she was, too, that in some irrational way she had waited for him all her life, even through the years before they'd met, but it was too late to talk, too late to think. His kiss was deepening, demanding her surrender, and she gave it willingly, her lips parting beneath his. His tongue stroked hers, moving within her mouth while his hand moved over her body, its calloused caress turning her to flame. He was murmuring her name, whispering things she only half heard, but it didn't matter. Words were nothing but unnecessary intrusions in the dreamworld they had created. She needed no words to learn the taste of Rhys's mouth or the feel of his hard body. She touched him hesitantly at first and then, as he moaned his pleasure, she touched him with increasing boldness, revelling in the feel of his muscled chest, his supple skin.

'You're so lovely,' he whispered. 'If you knew how I've dreamed of this, of kissing you like this...your breasts, your belly, every part of you...'

She gasped as his kisses covered her. 'Rhys,' she said, 'no...'

'Yes,' he said fiercely, 'yes.'

His breath was warm against the silken flesh of her thighs, his mouth hot. She arched against his hand, whimpering as he gently stroked her hidden moistness, and when his mouth finally found her, when she felt the touch of his lips and tongue, tears filled her eyes.

She wanted to cry out, to clasp him to her heart and say, Rhys, I love you—I'll always love you... because that was the truth, but there was another truth, one that still overshadowed everything else, one that she would have a lifetime to regret. There was nothing she could say, nothing she could do except give in to the wonder of what Rhys was teaching her. When finally he took her in his arms again, she could only cling to him and bury her face against his throat.

'Rhys,' she whispered brokenly, 'oh, Rhys...'

He put his fingers beneath her chin and lifted her face to his. 'Blair, sweet Blair,' he said as he kissed her, 'are you all right?'

'Yes,' she said, 'oh, yes. But you...'

He smiled at her. 'I'll be fine,' he said softly. 'You'll see.'

A tremor shot through her as his smile faded, and a dark intensity narrowed his eyes. She murmured his name as his mouth claimed hers with heated urgency, and her arms went around his neck, holding him tightly against her. His hands slid beneath her, lifting her to him, bringing her to his hard maleness. Blair cried out softly as he entered her, arching against him, and he paused, waiting as her body accepted his.

'Blair?' he whispered.

'Don't stop,' she breathed. 'Please...'

And, as Rhys began to move within her, as he took her upwards with him towards that precious instant when time stopped, when life itself seemed to cease and then began anew, Blair knew that nothing would ever be the same for her again.

CHAPTER ELEVEN

BLAIR awoke slowly, alone in the farmhouse bed. The scent of coffee drifted in through the half-open doorway and she smiled, thinking of how like that first morning this was—except that then Rhys had been her enemy, and now...now, she thought, her lashes falling to her cheeks as she remembered the long, sweet hours of the night, now he was her lover.

She sat up in bed and ran her fingers through her tousled hair. Nothing had prepared her for the wonder she'd found in Rhys's arms. They'd made love all through the night, the last time a dreamlike encounter when she'd awakened to the heated moistness of his mouth against the nape of her neck, the silken demand of his hands as they cupped her breasts. She'd started to turn in his arms, but Rhys had drawn her hips back against him and then he'd taken her on that breathless climb again, taken her to that moment when the light shattered beneath her closed eyelids, when her heart seemed so filled with love that she thought surely it would burst.

And he loved her, she thought, smiling sleepily. He didn't need to say it. She knew he did. His kisses, his caresses, even the way he'd held her in his arms had told her how he felt. All of which made it that much more difficult to tell him the long-overdue truth about herself, Blair thought as she swung her feet to the floor. She'd played through the scene in her mind at least a dozen times. Sometimes Rhys was furious. Other times, he retreated into a cold silence. But always the scene ended with his taking her in his arms and assuring her that he

158

loved her. That was the one certainty the night had brought.

She dressed quickly and ran her comb through her hair, peering at herself in the clouded mirror. Gently, she touched a finger to her swollen mouth. Rhys's kisses had done that, she thought, and a slow swell of heat spread upwards from her loins.

'Shameless woman,' she hissed at her reflection, and then she laughed aloud with pleasure.

But she paused in the doorway to the kitchen, suddenly shy as she saw Rhys sitting at the table. He was drinking coffee and he'd been reading a magazine—it was still there, in front of him. Blair took a breath and walked into the room.

'Good morning.'

He looked at her over the rim of his cup. The steam rising from it obscured his face.

'Good morning,' he said.

She waited for him to say something else, but there was only silence. Irrationally, Blair found herself thinking of the articles in women's magazines, things with titles like 'Small Talk the Morning After'. They'd always struck her as tasteless nonsense, but at this moment she wished she'd read them all. How could she feel so awkward in the presence of a man who knew her so intimately?

'The coffee smells good,' she said. 'I—er—I guess I overslept.' Still he said nothing. Finally, she turned away and padded to the stove. 'I see the rain's stopped,' she said brightly. 'I didn't expect today to be so sunny, did you?'

'Never expect anything,' he said. 'Life's simpler that way.'

The coffeepot trembled in her hand and she set it down carefully before she turned to face him. The cup was at his lips again but, as she watched, he lowered it and the cloudy haze dissipated, revealing eyes as flat and cold as his voice. Blair managed a smile.

'What's the matter?' she said. 'Have you got the early morning grumps?'

'Nothing's the matter,' he said in that same distant tone.

Suddenly her palms felt damp, and she ran them down her thighs, still keeping the smile plastered to her face. 'I know what it is,' she said with false good cheer. 'You were reading that magazine. Aunt Annie always says it's a mistake to try and deal with the news on an empty stomach. She says...'

His eyes flickered over her and then he got to his feet. 'I'd love to hear Aunt Annie's homilies, but I'm afraid we're pressed for time. I want to make that call to Rome while it's still early.'

A cold hand seemed to close around Blair's heart. 'Of course,' she whispered.

He put his cup in the sink and she watched his retreating back as he went into the bedroom. Could he have learned the truth about her? Her eyes widened and she put the back of her hand to her mouth. No, of course not. It was impossible.

'I'm gong to pack,' he said from the doorway. 'Just in case your father gives us the all clear.'

Your father, she thought. He wouldn't have referred to Oscar Desmond that way if he knew. Then what was it?

She looked at him and managed a shaky smile. 'My,' she said brightly, 'you're really in a rush, aren't you?'

His eyebrows rose. 'Ah, I see,' he said softly. 'You expected me to come back to bed, is that it?'

A dark blush rose to her cheeks. 'No,' she said quickly, 'that's not...'

'Good,' he said, interrupting her. 'Because the call to your father is really quite necessary.' His lips twisted in a quick smile. 'I'm sure you must be concerned about things back in Rome, Blair.'

She took a deep breath. She had envisioned telling him the truth differently, but she had put it off long enough. *Now,* she thought, and she took a step towards him.

'Yes,' she said quickly, 'yes, I certainly am, Rhys. I...' She laughed nervously. 'God, I wish I'd told you this sooner. I mean, it would have been simpler then. You see, I...I haven't been completely honest with you. I...'

'Haven't you?' he asked softly.

He was looking at her so strangely. There was a kind of reserve on his face, the sort of look you put on when you make small talk with strangers, except...except that it was like a mask hiding something else, something real—and suddenly she had the feeling that if she could see his face really see it—the blood would turn to ice in her veins.

'No,' she said carefully, 'I haven't. I...I wanted to tell you. I tried. I said I wasn't the woman you thought I was, I...' His eyes were turning darker, colder, and she took another breath. 'But then, after I began to feel that I...after I realised I wanted you to...to...'

'To make love to you,' he said coldly.

Colour flooded her cheeks. 'No...no, it wasn't that. I... I was afraid it would change everything if I told you the truth about myself,' she whispered lamely, forcing her eyes to meet his. 'For you, I mean. Not for me, of course...'

'I'm afraid you give me too much credit, Blair. I'd have taken you to bed sooner or later, no matter what you told me about yourself.' His eyes bored into hers, the irises like grey ice. 'You're a desirable woman, and under the circumstances—a man, a woman, living on the edge... It's happened before.'

What was he saying? The driving need to tell him about herself faded as she listened to him, as his words changed what had been a night of love into a cheap adventure. And now he was smiling, that quick, feral smile she remembered from the day he'd abducted her, and he was telling her it was too bad things had to end so quickly, that his need to return to Rome was as great as hers.

'I've got to be in Bahrain the day after tomorrow.'

'Bahrain?' she repeated dully.

He nodded as he walked towards the bedroom. 'We have a new operation to set up,' he said over his shoulder. 'I always tend to such things personally—I'll be gone for two or three months.' He picked up the carry-on and looked at her. 'It's nothing for you to worry about, of course.'

'Of course,' she said, watching as he stuffed things into the carry-on.

'If it's not safe to return to Rome yet, I'll make other arrangements for your security.' He turned away from her and bent over the carry-on. 'Any questions?'

Tears flooded Blair's eyes, but she fought against them. He had made her no promises, she reminded herself. He hadn't told her any lies; there had been no whispers of love or talk of a future during the dark night. And yet, she had been so sure...

'Yes,' she whispered finally. 'Just... just one. About last night...'

He paused, then hoisted the bag to his shoulder and turned to her. His face, she saw, was the face of a stranger. No, she thought suddenly, not a stranger. This cold, thin-lipped mask belong to the man named Hunter.

'Don't worry about it,' he said carefully. 'Discretion is part of my business.'

There was nothing left to say after that. They made the trip to Fiorello in silence. When they reached the phone booth, Blair turned to Hunter and held out her hand.

'Give me the tokens,' she said quietly. 'I'll make the call.'

Hunter nodded. 'Very well. If your father wants to talk to me...'

But she didn't give Oscar Desmond the opportunity. He answered the phone on the first ring; she turned her back on Hunter when she heard his gravelly voice.

'It's me,' she said. 'We're coming back.'

'Fine, fine,' Meryl's father rasped. 'Have you told Hunter anything?'

'No,' she whispered fiercely. 'And neither will you.' She hung up before he could say anything more, and stepped out into the August heat. 'Let's get going,' she told Hunter. 'They're expecting me.'

She feigned sleep during most of the long ride to Rome. Anything was better than looking at Hunter's impassive profile, or trying to make stilted conversation. Except for an occasional comment about the traffic or the weather, he was silent anyway. But, of course, his thoughts were already in Bahrain—he immersed himself in unusual cases, he'd said. That was why he'd taken on the Desmond case, she reminded herself. If only he hadn't. If only she and Meryl...

He pulled up before the iron gate of the Desmond villa in the late afternoon. There was an electric hum, the sound of static, and then a disembodied voice asked a question in Italian. Hunter answered, and after a few seconds the gate swung open and a man appeared.

'Jake will take you in,' Hunter said politely, 'if that's all right with you.'

'Of course,' Blair said, and then, without warning, her tightly held composure began to slip. She flung open the door and stepped into the blazing heat. 'Just tell me one thing, Hunter,' she said in a harsh whisper. 'Why have you treated me so carelessly?'

For a moment, his face paled. 'Carelessly?' he repeated. 'Is that what you think?'

She nodded. 'Yes,' she said, and then, to her horror, her eyes filled with tears. 'Yes, that's what I think.'

'Carelessly,' he repeated softly, and suddenly he reached across the car and grasped her wrist. 'You're lucky I didn't kill you.'

'Hunter, you're hurting me...'

He flung her from him and slammed the car into gear. 'That's the first good news I've heard all day,' he snarled, and then he was gone.

'You could at least try smiling once in a while,' Meryl said grumpily, collapsing on the velvet loveseat opposite Blair. 'Maids of honour are supposed to be cheerful.'

Blair sighed deeply. 'I'm not very good company, am I? I'm sorry, Meryl. I'll be all smiles tomorrow, I promise.'

'One of us had better be,' Meryl sniffed, tossing her magazine aside. 'I don't know—maybe I shouldn't have agreed to such a quick wedding. Maybe Perry and I should wait until we get back to Los Angeles. Maybe...'

'Don't be silly! You guys are crazy about each other. And the garden's a perfect setting for a wedding.' Blair leaned forward and patted her friend's hand. 'At least let me be grateful that one good thing came out of everything that happened last month.'

'I just wish I knew what *did* happen,' Meryl said softly. 'You came back here looking as if you wanted to die, and you've been as closed-mouth as a sprung trap ever since.'

Blair rose and walked across the room, pausing at the french doors. She watched absent-mindedly as workmen completed the final arrangements in the Desmond garden for the next day's nuptials. Irritation sharpened her voice when she spoke.

'Come on, Meryl. I've told you the story a dozen times. Hunter and I spent a few uncomfortable days living in a drafty old farmhouse near Florence. He thought I was you...'

'He still thinks it,' Meryl said gently. 'Why won't you let Daddy tell him the truth?'

'What's the difference? It's not as if he and I will ever set eyes on each other again, Hunter's in Bahrain...'

Wherever that is,' Meryl muttered.

'Exactly. And I'm here. By the time he gets back, you and I will be in the States again.'

Meryl grinned. 'Don't forget Perry.'

'How could I?' Blair asked with a quick smile. 'Every time I look up, there he is, drooling all over you.'

Meryl got to her feet and crossed the room to Blair's side. 'Don't knock it till you try it, kid,' she said softly.

'I didn't mean that. I...'

'I know you didn't. In fact, if I didn't know it was crazy, I'd swear you were carrying a torch for the mysterious Mr Hunter.' Meryl touched Blair's shoulder. 'That *is* crazy, isn't it? I mean, you didn't fall for the iceman, did you?'

'The iceman?'

Meryl shrugged. 'That's what Daddy calls him. He says it's one of the reasons Hunter's so effective—you know, that he has no emotions.' She gave Blair a sidelong glance. 'Or is Daddy wrong?'

A blush spread across Blair's cheeks. 'I don't know what you're talking about. I...'

'You're really a terrible liar, you know that?' Meryl sighed and put her arm around Blair's shoulders. 'Something happened to you while you were with Hunter. I just wish you'd confide in me.'

Blair pulled away from her employer's hand. 'Yes, all right,' she said suddenly, 'something did. But there's no point in talking about it. You can't help me. Nobody can. I...' Her voice broke and she turned her face away.

'Oh, lord...' Meryl's eyebrows rose in disbelief. 'You're in love with him,' she said softly. 'Really in love with him, I mean.'

Perhaps it was the scent of the orange blossoms banked in the adjoining library, or the gaily striped tent the caterers were even now raising in the garden. Whatever it was, three weeks of denial, of light-hearted anecdotes about the days she'd spent playing at being Meryl Desmond, came to a crashing halt. Blair leaned her forehead against the french doors.

'Yes,' she admitted in a tremulous whisper, 'I'm in love with him.'

Meryl watched her in stunned silence, and then she drew in her breath. 'I knew it was something,' she murmured. 'I thought it was a crush. You know, just one of those things that happens.'

'*One* of those things that happens describes it perfectly,' Blair said bitterly. 'It was all one-sided. I fell in love with him, but he didn't fall in love with me.'

'You mean, you told him how you felt and he...'

'No, no, of course not. But he...' Her eyes clouded with the memory of that last morning. 'He made it clear enough,' she finished quietly.

'Why? What did he say? What happened?'

'Nothing,' Blair sighed. 'It's...it's hard to explain. I woke up and went into the kitchen that last morning and he was sitting there, drinking coffee and reading.' Her glance roved across the room. 'Reading a magazine like that, as a matter of fact. And he...he simply said...he said it had been nice knowing me, but he had to get back to work.'

'Just like that?'

She nodded. 'Close enough. And then...and then when he dropped me off here, at the villa, he said something...he said something so awful, so cruel...'

'What?'

Blair took a breath. 'He said... he said I was lucky he hadn't kil...' She swallowed and shook her head. 'It doesn't matter. He just reverted to type, that's all. He's a strange man, Meryl. Hard, do you know what I mean? Unyielding...'

'Yes, I know what you mean,' Meryl said grimly. 'He's a bastard. And he can just go find himself another employer. I'll tell my father not to renew his contract.'

Blair shook her head. 'No, please, don't do that.' Her eyes sought Meryl's. 'He's good at what he does,' she said softly. 'I... I never felt safer in my life than when I was with him.'

Meryl Desmond's eyes brimmed with sudden understanding. 'Poor baby,' she whispered.

Blair lifted her chin. 'I'll get over it.'

'Of course you will,' her employer said with false good cheer. 'Just wait until you see the gorgeous waiters the caterer uses. Why, if Perry's not careful, I may just substitute one of them!'

Blair laughed and wiped her hand roughly across her eyes. 'Not if I see him first,' she said, linking her arm through Meryl's. 'Now, come on and give me another peek at that dress of yours. I don't think I've ever seen anything lovelier.'

It was all the wedding preparations that had finally got to her, Blair thought late that evening as she let herself quietly into the garden behind the villa. It was as Meryl had said: she'd been a bit subdued since Hunter had returned her to Rome, but she'd managed to keep up a pretty good front. It hadn't been too difficult, actually. Oscar Desmond had never met her before, and Meryl had been busy arranging the wedding that had apparently gone into the planning stage the very day Blair had been 'abducted'. Oh, Meryl had teased her about Hunter and all the the time they'd spent alone together, but Blair had managed to shrug off all her questions—until today.

Until today, she thought again, staring into the shadowed garden. But, today, the blue and white wedding tent had risen against the dark green cypresses; today, the caterer had wheeled in a four-tier cake with a tiny bride and groom perched on top; today, Meryl had pirouetted before the mirror in her antique lace wedding dress, a look of such bliss on her face that Blair's heartache had become suddenly more than she could bear.

It was foolish, romantic nonsense, that's all it was. Hunter had never spoken of love or commitment. He'd whispered of desire and pleasure, yes, and he'd given her that, God, he had, he had...

She shivered as a nightingale called softly from the rear of the garden. He'd looked so amazed when she'd accused him of treating her so carelessly—and then he'd said she was lucky he hadn't killed her. It had made no sense then and it made none now, weeks later, but the memory of how he'd looked when he'd said it, the coldness in his silver eyes, the twist to his mouth—she would never forget any of it. She still awoke in the dark night, her heart pounding, remembering his face, his words, the whispered threat.

She looked up as the nightingale called again. The answer was to forget Hunter, forget everything he'd said and done. She dug her hands into the pockets of her cotton skirt as she started along the gravel path leading to a reflecting pool in the cypress grove. She'd tried, heaven knew. She'd let Perry talk her into going out on a double date with his best man, a perfectly nice boy who'd flown over from the States. But he was a boy, not a man, certainly not a man like Hunter, and when he'd kissed her goodnight, the touch of his lips had only reminded her that no man had ever kissed her the way Hunter had, that no man had ever touched her as he had, that just thinking of him could make her tremble.

'Stop it,' she said.

Her voice seemed unnaturally loud in the silent garden,
and she shivered again. It was getting dark quickly; she
thought she remembered this area being illuminated, that
there were lights set in among the cypresses, but it was
dark. Perhaps the workmen had disconnected a wire or
something... A sudden, hot wind rustled through the
trees and the branches made a sound that was strangely
like a moan. Blair paused and looked around her. The
garden was a cheerful place by day, but it seemed ominous now, the trees tall and black against the inky sky,
the moon caught in the branches of a pine that stood
lonely on the Janiculum Hill overlooking the city.
Something called out in the darkness, something small
and frightened, and the hair rose on the back of Blair's
neck.

She turned quickly and faced the villa. She could see
its lights gleaming brightly, beckoning to her cheerfully
through the shadows. She squared her shoulders and
lifted her chin. She was letting her imagination run away
with her. Don't go out of the villa alone, Meryl's father
had warned them both, and neither girl had, but there
were no restrictions against walking the grounds. There
were guards and dogs and all kinds of electronic gadgets,
the kind Hunter had told her about, and...

A pair of strong arms snaked around her from the
rear, enclosing her like the coils of a python, one hard-
muscled coil lying just beneath her breasts, the other
resting lightly against her throat. Blair opened her mouth
to scream, but a hand closed over her mouth, a large,
leather-gloved hand that pressed firmly against her lips.
Terror flooded through her, turning her legs to jelly.

'Not a sound.' The man's voice was a toneless whisper
against her ear; his breath was warm as it stirred the hair
on the side of her head. 'Do you understand me?' Fear
made her rigid. He repeated the question and Blair
nodded. 'Good. If you do as you're told, you'll be all
right.'

She nodded again. Her heart was thumping crazily in her chest; she wondered if the intruder could feel the leap of her pulse beneath his wrist. She was pressed tightly against him, her weight tilted back so that most of it was on her heels. It was a position that made it impossible for her to run or struggle. She could feel the hard, muscled length of him pressing into her from thigh to shoulder. His heartbeat was slow and strong beneath her ear, but the rasp of his breath was ragged, as if he'd been running. His lips brushed her earlobe again.

'There's a gate in the rear of the cypress grove,' he whispered. 'Do you know it? She nodded once more. Yes, she knew the gate. She'd found it one day by accident. It was old, rusted from disuse and overgrown with creeping tendrils of ivy. 'We're going out that way,' he murmured. His words made her stiffen, and he drew her even more closely against him. 'You'll be all right if you behave. I don't want to hurt you, but I will if you give me the slightest cause. Do you understand?'

Blair nodded again. A chill danced along her flesh as the intruder's arms curled around her waist. 'Move,' he ordered, bringing her tightly into the hard curve of his body as he led her deeper into the grove. 'Not a sound,' he warned, his lips pressed to her ear.

Her heart tripped within her chest as he spoke. The heat of his breath against her skin made her tremble, but this time with something that was not quite terror. For Blair had suddenly put a name to the sound of the whispered voice and the feel of the powerful body pressed against hers.

It was Hunter.

CHAPTER TWELVE

THE rusted gate swung open easily—so easily that Blair knew it had been tampered with. Hunter slipped through the tangle of ivy and drew her into the street that curved behind the villa. His hand lay hot and heavy against her ribs, his fingers like steel rode just beneath her breast. The hot August night was silent around them, tense and expectant.

Blair stumbled to a halt as the gate closed soundlessly behind them. The narrow, cobblestoned street was empty. Not even one of Rome's omnipresent street cats, out scavenging a night-time meal, was visible. *Even the cats are afraid to show themselves...* It was an irrational thought, but tendrils of fear were spreading within Blair's mind like the searching roots of an evil flower.

'Move,' Hunter rasped.

She began to do as he'd ordered, and then she spotted the silver Lamborghini at the kerb. For a moment, she almost laughed aloud. He wasn't doing a very good job of disguising himself. Was all this some kind of insane game?

'Hunter,' she said, 'I know it's you.'

His laughter was soft and unpleasant. 'Clever girl,' he whispered, pulling her back against him until her head rested beneath his chin. 'Now, do as I tell you. Get moving.'

Her heart thudded against her ribs. 'This is crazy,' she said. 'It's...'

His arm tightened around her. 'When I want your opinion, I'll ask for it. Go on, get into the car.'

'No,' she whispered, dragging her feet against the uneven cobblestones. 'No, I won't, I . . .'

'Do it!'

Her heart thudded again, and she hurried to obey the snarling command. All right, she thought, it wasn't a game, not that she'd really believed it could be. Hunter didn't play at things like this—no one knew that better than she. And there was no point in trying to get away as he crossed to the driver's side of the car. He was faster than she was and much, much stronger—no one knew *that* better than she. The memory of the first time he'd abducted her was still as fresh as if it had happened yesterday.

She watched as he stabbed the key into the ignition and pressed down hard on the accelerator. What was he up to? There had been a logical reason when he'd carried her off at the airport. He'd been trying to save her— well, trying to save Meryl Desmond—from harm. That was why he'd snatched her then . . .

Was that it? Was something terrible happening at the villa? Yes, she thought, yes, of course. That was why Hunter had taken her away so quickly. There hadn't been any time for explanations or . . .

She glanced over her shoulder, half expecting to see someone following them, and Hunter laughed.

'Don't bother looking. There won't be anyone back there.'

'Yes, but if something's going on at the villa . . .' He looked at her, his raised eyebrows visible in the headlights of an oncoming car. 'Isn't that why . . .' Blair's voice faltered. 'Isn't that why you did this? Because there was danger?'

He laughed again and looked back at the road. 'With three Rottweilers patrolling the grounds, half a dozen infra-red videocams and trip beams criss-crossing every access point? No, nothing's happening at the villa, Blair.' He looked at her and his teeth flashed whitely. 'Just wedding preparations,' he said softly. 'And there's nothing dangerous about that, is there?'

She looked away from him and stared into the darkness. 'Then why are you doing this, Hunter? What do you want from me?'

He shifted into higher gear as they reached the open road. 'Settle back and relax, Blair. You've probably had a busy day—weddings take a lot of effort, don't they?'

His voice was low and soothing, but it did nothing to calm her. He was talking to her as if she were a child or an incompetent, she thought, and the anger began to grow within her.

'You can't get away with this, Hunter,' she said. 'You can't just . . . just kidnap somebody.'

The car picked up speed as the black Italian countryside gathered them in.

'Just settle down and take it easy. No one's going to miss you for quite a while, and by the time they do . . .'

'They'll call the police,' she said angrily. 'Has that occurred to you? The roads will be crawling with cops before you get a chance to do . . . to do whatever it is you're doing. You may have gotten away with kidnapping me last time, but you won't be able to do it twice.'

He turned to her and laughed. 'Just watch me, Miss Desmond. I've planned it right down to the final detail.' His laughter died abruptly. 'And I don't leave anything to chance,' he said coldly. 'You should know that by now. So just sit back . . .'

'Damn you, Hunter,' she said furiously, 'stop telling me that! I want to know why you abducted me. What do you want?'

He turned his face to hers. She could see nothing but his eyes, those cold silver flames burning within his shadowed face, and her throat constricted with fear.

'Are you sure you really want to know?'

Was this the man she was in love with? she thought, staring into his hard face. She must have been crazy! He was—he was just what Meryl had called him. He was an iceman. Worse than that. He was the sum of all the things he'd said he'd been—a soldier, a spy, a man who would do what he had to do and then justify it with some chauvinistic code of honour.

Her throat constricted with fear. 'No,' she whispered, 'no, I don't want to know. I just want you to turn this car around and take me back.'

'We're not going back.'

She knew that flat, steel-grey tone, she thought, closing her eyes. When he sounded that way, she knew there was no changing his mind about anything. Still, she had to try. She shifted towards him, turning her face to him.

'Hunter,' she said carefully, 'please, just listen. You...'

His mouth tightened. 'Shut up.'

'Dammit, Hunter...'

'You're boring me, Blair.'

He reached towards the cassette player set into the dashboard. Within seconds, the dramatic opening chords of Beethoven's *Fifth Symphony* filled the car.

'I can't talk over that noise,' she said. 'Can't you turn it down?'

But noise was exactly what he'd wanted. Each time she opened her mouth, he increased the volume of the tape. Finally, when her eardrums couldn't take another decibel, she clamped her lips together and sat back in stony silence.

She had no idea where they were or in what direction they were headed. Darkness and the speed of the Lamborghini were as effective as a blindfold. And there was no point in asking him, even if he turned down the music. She glanced at him in the light of an incoming car. There he sat, dressed in black cords and a black turtleneck shirt despite the heat, with that damned impassive profile that said more clearly than words ever could that he'd tell her what he wanted, when he wanted. It didn't matter a damn to him that he was frightening the life out of her, that he was intimidating her—that he'd whisked her away on the very eve of the wedding...

The sudden realisation brought a quick, satisfied smile to her face. Rhys Hunter, the great security expert, still didn't know he'd snatched the wrong woman—and he'd done it not once, but twice. Blair risked a quick look at him. Go on, she thought, play at being a midnight commando! You just wait until we get wherever we're going. I'll tell you who I really am. I'll tell you how stupid you are! Yes, she thought, settling back in the seat, that would take care of Mr Hunter. A few weeks ago, she'd worried about wounding his pride. Now, she relished the thought of destroying it.

The car raced on into the night. Gradually, she began to realise there was only one place he could be taking her. Not to Florence—they'd have to be on the road too long for that and, no matter what he said, he'd have to worry about the authorities this time. The villa he'd taken her to the day he'd abducted her from the airport, then. That had to be where they were going.

It was. The Lamborghini swung sharply to the right and mounted the rise leading to the small stand of cypresses standing darkly against the night sky. Hunter touched something on the dash and the garage door swung open. He shut off the engine as soon as they were inside the building, and the door hissed closed behind them.

'OK,' he said softly. 'Out.'

Blair took a deliberate breath. 'Hunter, for the last time...'

'I hope so,' he said, wrenching open her door. 'I'm getting tired of listening to you. Now, get out. You know the way.'

She gritted her teeth and swung her legs from the car. There was no sense in arguing with him now, not when there was nothing she could do but follow his orders. Later, perhaps, when they weren't in such close quarters, there might be a chance to ignore his instructions, a chance to get away. For now, all she could do was obey.

She marched ahead of him to the door, waiting while he unlocked it, and then she stepped inside the dark house. A switch clicked on the wall beside her and Blair blinked in the sudden flood of light. Hunter cursed softly and touched the switch again, and the light dimmed to a soft glow.

Blair had been too frightened to really look around her the last time she'd been in the villa. She was still frightened, but this time she was determined to use every moment to good advantage. She moved forwards slowly, taking a careful survey of the room in which they stood, hoping for some miraculous means of escape to present itself.

The room was large, its predominant colours a muted charcoal and a pale cream. Thick carpet covered the floor. A pair of couches flanked a free-standing brick fireplace; beyond there was a long window wall overhung by vertical blinds in a fabric that matched the couches. Shelves marched up the near wall, most of them covered with books, except for the middle one, which housed a compact disc player and other sound equipment. The light came from recessed overhead spotlights. A book lay, open and face down, on one of the couches. All in all, it was a handsome room, a comfortable room, and Hunter, leaning casually against one of the pale walls, looked very much at home in it.

'Satisfied?'

His voice was cool and mocking. Blair squared her shoulders. Somehow, she sensed it was important not to let him know how frightened she was.

'Is that why you brought me here? To admire your decorating scheme?'

He tossed his keys on a table that stood near the door. 'The windows are double-glazed and mirrored,' he said casually, strolling across the room and pulling back the vertical blinds as he spoke. 'They're virtually impossible to smash. The view from here is magnificent, Blair.' He drew the blinds closed and smiled coldly. 'You could stand at that window for hours and see nothing in the valley below except an occasional wild boar.'

She felt her pulse leap. 'I don't know why you're telling me all this, Hunter. I...'

'Yes, you do. You were checking this room like a weasel caught down the wrong burrow. I'm just trying to save you a hell of a lot of trouble. You can't get out the door, either. I've closed it electronically—you'd have to punch in the right series of numbers to get it to open for you.' He smiled again. 'You'd get it right eventually—give or take a hundred years.'

Don't let him see that you're afraid, Blair...

'All right,' she said, 'you've had your fun and games. Now take me back to Rome.'

A quick smile came and went on his face. 'When I'm good and ready.'

Her chin rose. 'Hunter, you'd better listen to me. There are things I could say to you, things you don't want to hear...'

His eyes darkened. 'Funny,' he said softly, 'that was going to be my line.'

'What are you talking about? There's nothing you could say that would upset me. I...'

'Isn't there?' he asked softly.

Dear lord, she thought, her eyes widening. Was he going to tell her he'd kidnapped her for ransom? It was the only thing that made sense.

'I really misjudged you, Hunter,' she said quietly.

His eyes swept over her, his gaze lingering on the rapid rise and fall of her breasts. 'Yes,' he said, his voice a low whisper, 'yes, you did.'

She swallowed past the sudden lump in her throat. 'How much are you going to ask for me?' she demanded.

His eyes narrowed. 'How much am I . . .'

'Come on, Hunter,' she said, hoping she sounded tougher than she felt, 'I'm not stupid. I'm just surprised you suddenly decided it was more profitable to steal people than it was to protect them. I . . .'

The breath caught in her throat as he moved towards her. Anger darkened his face; she flinched away as his hand encircled her wrist and drew her forward.

'You really don't know the first goddamned thing about honour, do you?' The low timbre of his voice sent tremors of fear through her; his face was so close to hers that she could see a muscle twitch beneath the skin of his cheek. 'Is that what you think this is all about?'

His fingers were biting into the tender flesh on the underside of her wrist, but she held her ground.

'You said . . . you said you were going to tell me something that would upset me, and I thought . . . I figured . . .'

'Does your fiancé know what a bitch you really are, Blair? Or am I the only one who's had the privilege of getting to know the real Meryl Blair Desmond?'

Blair swallowed. 'Listen, Hunter—about that. You've made an awful mistake . . .'

His eyes smiled coldly into hers. 'Have I?'

'Ye-yes,' she breathed as he drew her closer to him. 'You see, I'm not . . . I never was . . .'

'No,' he said softly, 'you never were. I just wonder if you're everything poor old Perry what's-his-name thinks you are.'

'Perry's got nothing to do with this. . . .'

His hand tightened on hers. 'What's he like, Blair? An attorney, the magazine said. Is that right?'

'He's . . . yes, I guess that's what he is. I . . .'

His head dropped towards hers. 'You guess? Don't you know?'

'He...he works for his father. They own a chain of stores, and Perry's in charge of the legal end... Listen, Hunter, they'll know I'm gone by now. There's a midnight supper at the villa, did you know that? Everybody will be looking for me...'

His eyes burned into hers. 'Nobody even knows I took you,' he said in a soft whisper. 'Did *you* know that?'

Her heart banged loudly. 'Your men know, don't they?' she asked in a raspy whisper. 'I mean, how else could you have sneaked into the grounds?'

His smile sent a chill deep into the marrow of her bones. 'I told you, Blair. I'm good at what I do. Damned good.' His eyes narrowed as he looked into her face. 'No one knows I took you,' he repeated. His free hand slid up her back and curled around the nape of her neck. 'I can do anything I want to you,' he said softly, 'and no one would know.'

She couldn't breathe. She couldn't swallow. She could only look into Hunter's face and wonder what she had done to make him hate her with such all-consuming passion. Thank God she hadn't told him the truth about herself a moment ago, she thought with a shudder. *If I trust you and you let me down,* he'd said... If he felt this way about her now, how would he feel if he knew she'd lied and cheated from the moment they'd met?

Blair ran her tongue over her dry lips. 'Wh-what are you going to do?' she whispered finally.

Hunter's eyes became blank. His fingers loosened on her neck, his thumb moving over her skin in what was almost a caress.

'I don't know,' he said after a long silence. His fingers tangled in her hair and he forced her face up to his. 'I don't know, Blair,' he repeated and his head lowered towards hers.

'No,' she said, trying to turn away from him, 'no, Hunter, don't...'

His mouth closed over hers with a punishing passion that drove the breath from her. Tears stung her eyelids as she thought of the last time he'd kissed her, on that long-ago night in the Tuscan hills, when they'd lain in each other's arms and she'd let herself think he loved her.

His mouth gentled on hers. His lips were asking now, not demanding, his tongue offering, not insisting. And suddenly she was drowning in that same pool of liquid fire she'd known in his arms before, clinging to him, murmuring his name as his arms closed around her...

Hunter thrust her from him. 'Jesus!' he whispered.

Blair stared at him, her eyes wide with shock. 'Keep away from me,' she said. 'I warn you, Hunter, I...' She pounded her fists against his chest as he swung her into his arms. 'Dammit, what are you doing? Hunter? Hunter! Where are you taking me?'

'Where I can keep you until I decide what the hell to do with you,' he growled as he carried her through the house. He kicked open a door and hit the light switch with his elbow. 'The glass is double-glazed in here, too,' he said, dumping her on the floor. 'Don't even bother trying to get out.'

She looked around her wildly. She was in a small bedroom; Hunter was already stepping into the hall and closing the door after him.

'Hunter...'

He paused and gave her one last, long look. 'Maybe we're both sick,' he said softly. 'And it's either quarantine or Coventry before we destroy each other.'

The door slammed, and Blair was alone.

She had slept. She had no idea for how long, but when she opened her eyes she felt headachey and stiff. But she would be, lying on the edge of the bed this way... She drew in her breath and sat up quickly as everything that had happened came rushing back to her. Hunter had left her and she'd pounded on the door until finally she'd slipped to the floor, sobbing with frustration, and then she'd stumbled to the bed and sat down on it, determined to outwait him.

And she'd fallen asleep. Such a prosaic thing to do while a madman lurked outside, she thought with a bitter smile. It was late, and the night had turned black and chill. Blair wrapped her arms around herself and shuddered. There was a blanket on the bed, but she'd be damned if she'd use it. She wouldn't use anything that belonged to Hunter, to that madman...

Her shoulders slumped in defeat. He wasn't mad. She knew that. In fact, if anybody was crazy, it was she. Look at the way she'd behaved when he'd kissed her. Her eyes closed against the humiliating memory. It hadn't been a real kiss—he'd only done it to prove something. Maybe he was trying to remind her that he was stronger than she. Maybe he'd been trying to frighten her. Maybe he'd simply wanted to embarrass her by reminding her of what had been between them once. Whatever the reason, it was she who had melted in his embrace, she who had deepened the kiss, she who had clung to him as if she were drowning in that flood of sweet fire that flamed through her at his touch...

What time was it, anyway? She glanced at her wristwatch and blanched. It was almost five in the morning— the wedding was scheduled for nine. Perry had wanted a sunrise ceremony, but Meryl had laughed and insisted that nine a.m. was as close to sunrise as she was ever going to get in her life. She'd never be there in time, not even if she could talk Hunter into letting her go. It was at least a two-hour drive back to Rome, and she'd have to fix her hair and do her make-up and...

She bit back hysterical laughter. There wouldn't be a wedding, not if the police were crawling all over the Desmond villa. And surely they were, by now. They might even have picked up Hunter's trail—if, by some miracle, he'd left one. They could be surrounding his villa at this very moment, moving in on him while he slept, setting up rifles and guns and...

The police. The last time she'd thought about them in connection with Hunter was that day in Fiorello. She'd thought he was a kidnapper then, but she'd been willing to do anything to keep him safe... And she still would, she thought, as tears filled her eyes. Oh God, what was the matter with her? Hunter had seduced her and abandoned her, and now he'd stolen her for who knew what reason—and still she loved him. There was no sense in trying to deny it. She loved him, even though she didn't understand why he was so determined to hurt her even more than he already had.

She sprang to her feet as a key grated in the lock. The bedroom door swung open and Hunter stepped into the room. Dark shadows lay like bruises beneath his eyes. They looked at each other in silence, and then he let out his breath.

'All right,' he said. 'I'll take you back.'

A weight seemed to lift from her heart. 'Thank you,' she said, smiling at him through her tears. 'Thank you, Hunter.'

He nodded. 'There's not anything else I can do,' he said, as if to himself. His voice was hoarse with exhaustion. 'I...I don't know why I took you from the villa. I...'

He sounded so tired, she thought. And he looked so unhappy. She took a deep breath, fighting against the sudden desire to walk to his side and touch him.

'It's all right,' she said softly. 'We'll be back in time, if we hurry. And I won't tell anyone what happened. I...'

'Won't tell anyone? You'll have to tell Perry something, won't you? Dammit, Blair, the man's going to ask questions.'

She blinked. For a moment, she'd forgotten he still thought she was Meryl Desmond. Well, there was nothing to gain by telling him the truth now. She smiled at him and shrugged her shoulders.

'I . . . I'll think of something,' she murmured.

Hunter's eyes narrowed. 'You'll think of something?' he repeated.

Blair nodded. 'Yes. I'll tell him I . . . I was with friends. I'll tell him I was with . . . with . . .' Her voice broke and she turned away from him. 'I'll tell him I was with someone who's very important to me.'

She gasped as Hunter's hands closed on her shoulders. He spun her towards him and drew her forwards.

'And what will you tell him when he asks who made you a woman, Blair?' His voice, his face, were hard with anger. 'Well? I'm waiting for your answer, dammit. What will you tell him then?'

She looked at him in disbelief. 'I . . . I won't tell him anything, Hunter. He won't ask me.'

His fingers bit into her flesh. 'What do you mean, he won't ask you?' His eyes flamed to silver ice as they met hers. 'Doesn't he love you? Doesn't he want to know that your heart and body belong only to him?'

'Hunter, please, you're hurting me . . .'

'Answer me,' he growled, shaking her as if she were a rag doll. 'Come on, Blair, answer me! Doesn't the man you're marrying love you even half as much as I do?'

In the sudden silence, Blair could hear only the rapid beat of her own pulse. She looked into Hunter's face, trying to decide if she had dreamed the words.

'What?' she whispered finally. 'What did you say?'

Hunter made a harsh sound in his throat. 'I said that the son of a bitch I'm bringing you back to had better love you or I'll kill him. You can tell him that for me, Blair. Tell him I said that I'll kill him if I ever even suspect he doesn't love you and want you and . . .'

The beat of her heart stumbled. 'Because...because you love me?'

'Of course I love you,' he growled. He bent his head to hers and stared at her. 'What did you think that last night at the farmhouse was all about, dammit? I'd already told you I loved you in a dozen different ways, and then that morning...' His hands dropped to his sides. 'What's the difference?' he growled. 'Look, it's getting late. We've got to get started if we're going to get you to the villa on time.'

Blair shook her head. 'I'm not leaving here until you tell me what you're talking about. What about that morning?'

'I told you, it doesn't matter.'

Her chin lifted. 'It does,' she said with quiet determination. 'I have a right to know.'

He sighed and ran his fingers through his hair. 'There was a stack of magazines in the back of the Land Rover, remember? I woke up that morning, put the coffee on, and went outside to check the area. And you...' His voice thickened, and he cleared his throat. 'You were curled up in the centre of the bed like a kitten... Hell, I knew what would have happened if I went back into that bedroom. And I knew we had to phone Rome. So I decided to play it safe. I grabbed the most recent magazine—I think it was the day before's—and took it into the kitchen to read while I waited for the coffee.'

His words drifted into silence and Blair took a step forwards. 'And?' she asked softly, although she knew, in her heart she knew...

Hunter's face darkened. 'It was a rag—one of those things that specialises in gossip. I started to put it aside—but a name jumped out at me.' His mouth twisted with pain. 'Your name,' he whispered. 'Meryl Desmond makes wedding plans,' it said, or something like that. I read it and re-read it and there was a picture of you at a nightclub back home with some guy called Perry, and...'

Tears of happiness welled in Blair's eyes. 'Hunter,' she whispered, 'please, you have to listen to me...'

His hands clasped her shoulders. 'You came out of the bedroom and said you hadn't been honest with me and... I wanted to kill you, Blair. I couldn't believe you didn't feel the way I did. Jesus, it was the one thing I'd have staked my life on.' He drew her towards him. 'Didn't that night mean anything to you?' he demanded in a gruff whisper.

There was so much to understand, so much to turn over in her mind and cherish. He had read an article and thought she was engaged to be married. That was the gist of it. But only one thing that he'd said really mattered. He loved her—Hunter loved her. Rhys loved her.

'Tell me why you brought me here, Rhys,' she whispered.

He gave her a quick, bitter smile. 'Who the hell knows? I didn't have this planned to the last detail—that was a lie. I had some insane idea I could change your mind about this Perry guy. I kept telling myself it was me you loved, not him.'

She thought of what he'd said about making her a woman. 'Because I gave you my virginity?' she asked softly.

A look of pain crossed his face. 'Because you gave me your heart,' he growled. 'At least, I thought you had...'

For the first time in weeks, Blair smiled. 'Aunt Annie wouldn't argue with that,' she said.

'Jesus, I don't give a damn about Aunt Annie right now, Blair. I...'

'She'd side with you, Rhys. And I'm sure she wouldn't want me to marry Perry, either.'

He gave her a strange look. 'She wouldn't?'

'She'd probably hope that I'd marry you.'

Rhys drew in his breath. 'Would she really?' he asked softly, his eyes searching hers.

Blair nodded. 'Well, she'd at least want me to consider your proposal, if you made one.' She tilted her head to the side and looked up at him. 'Were you going to make one?'

A hesitant smile caught at the corner of Hunter's mouth and then he scowled. 'Don't play games with me,' he said softly. 'I've told you that before.'

Blair breathed a silent prayer and then looked into Hunter's eyes. 'I've only played one game with you,' she said in a low voice. 'And I've regretted it almost since it began. That morning—that morning, when I started to tell you I hadn't been honest with you...' Her hands rose between them and she put her palms against his chest. 'It had nothing to do with Perry,' she said. 'You see, I ... I've never been engaged to him. I've never been engaged to anyone.' She felt the sudden surge of his heart beneath her hand. 'There isn't any easy way to tell you this, Rhys. I'll just have to come right out with it.'

His eyes narrowed. 'Dammit, come right out with what?'

She took a breath. 'Rhys, I...I'm not Meryl Desmond. That's what I meant when I said I hadn't been honest with you.'

'You're not Meryl Desmond?' His eyes never left hers as she shook her head. 'Then who...?'

'I'm Blair Nolan, Meryl's secretary. She and I switched passports and airplane tickets and...' Her voice broke and she swallowed hard.

Rhys's fingers bit into her arms. 'You mean, you lied to me all along?'

'I thought you were a kidnapper, and I was afraid to tell you I wasn't Meryl. I thought you'd kill me if you knew you couldn't ransom me off to Oscar Desmond.'

He shook his head in disbelief. 'But the next day, Blair. We called Rome. Hell, Desmond spoke to me. He spoke to you. He said I was to keep you out of sight...'

Her head fell forwards. 'That's the part I'm most ashamed of. He told me the *paparazzi* had no idea Meryl and her fiancé were at the villa. He said the privacy was wonderful. He begged me to... to go on pretending to be his daughter. He said you'd never agree to go along with the scheme if you knew the truth...'

'And you agreed?'

She nodded. 'I agreed,' she admitted, her eyes pleading for understanding. 'Try and see my side of it. Meryl is my friend. And Desmond made it sound as if my job might be on the line...' Her voice drifted off; when she spoke again, it was a whisper. 'There was another reason, too, one I was ashamed to admit to myself at first.'

Rhys put his hand beneath her chin and coaxed her head up. 'Tell me,' he said softly.

Her eyes met his. 'I ... I wanted to be with you. And then, after I knew I was... after I knew I was falling in love with you, I tried to tell you the truth. But... but I didn't have the courage. I was afraid you'd look at me the way you're looking at me now...'

'Why didn't you tell me that morning?' he demanded. 'How could you have let me think you belonged to another man?'

Tears glistened on her lashes. 'I thought you just wanted to get rid of me, that you'd... you had what you wanted from me...'

Rhys's eyes were fierce. 'Never,' he said.

'Yes, I know that now, but then... I'm so sorry,' she whispered, closing her eyes against the anger she saw in his. 'I don't blame you if you can't forgive me. You trusted me, and I let you down. Don't you see? That's why I couldn't tell you. I let you down. I...'

He cupped her face in his hands and raised it to his. 'I love you, Blair,' he said softly. 'I've never said that to anyone before. Do you understand? I love you. I'd trust you with my life.'

The tears spilled down her cheeks. 'Rhys, my love...'

He smiled down at her. 'Of course, I should put you over my knee and spank you.' He brushed a kiss lightly across her mouth. 'I'll bet Aunt Annie would approve.'

Blair laughed through her tears. 'She would, indeed.'

'Is there really an Aunt Annie, or is she just a figment of your imagination?'

'She's real as rain. Everything I told you about myself was the truth, Rhys. Everything but my name.'

His arms tightened around her. 'Tell me the only thing that matters,' he whispered. 'I want to hear you say it.'

'I love you,' she sighed, leaning back in his arms and smiling up at him. 'I'll always love you.'

He drew her against him again. 'What a mess we made of things,' he murmured.

'Did you really go to Bahrain?'

He laughed softly. 'I pulled one of my best men off a plane five minutes before flight time because I was sure I could lose myself in a new job. But it didn't work; as the day of the wedding got closer, I got nastier, and yesterday I finally said goodbye, Bahrain, and got myself out of there before someone shot me in self-defence!'

Blair looked up at him. 'Rhys? You still haven't said whether you've forgiven me...'

His eyebrows drew together in a dark scowl. 'I don't know,' he said slowly. 'I'll have to have some time to think about it.'

She nodded. 'Yes, I understand.'

Rhys glanced at his watch. 'But we'll have to talk about it later if you want to get back to the Desmond villa in time for the wedding.'

She shook her head. 'I... I don't want to do anything until I know.'

Rhys sighed. 'You are the most difficult woman, Blair Nolan. All right, there's no time for beating around the bush. So here it is. I love you. I'm going to marry you. And I want to meet Aunt Annie as soon as possible.' He grinned down at her. 'Now can we leave for Rome?'

Blair smiled. 'How long does it take to get to Rome from here?' she asked.

'About two hours. If we leave now, we'll make it with half an hour to spare.'

Blair's arms curled around Rhys's neck. 'I've got a better use for that half-hour,' she whispered.

And so had he.

Harlequin Presents

Coming Next Month

Available in April wherever paperback books are sold, or through Harlequin Reader Service:

In the U.S.
901 Fuhrmann Blvd.
P.O. Box 1397
Buffalo, N.Y. 14240-1397

In Canada
P.O. Box 603
Fort Erie, Ontario
L2A 5X3

Harlequin Regency Romance™

Romance the way it was *always* meant to be!

The time is 1811, when a Regent Prince rules the empire. The place is London, the glittering capital where rakish dukes and dazzling debutantes scheme and flirt in a dangerously exciting game. Where marriage is the passport to wealth and power, yet every girl hopes secretly for love....

Welcome to Harlequin Regency Romance where reading is an adventure and romance is *not* just a thing of the past! Two delightful books a month, beginning May '89.

Available wherever Harlequin Books are sold.

REG-1

◆ Harlequin Superromance

**Here are the longer, more involving stories you
have been waiting for... Superromance.**

Modern, believable novels of love, full of the complex
joys and heartaches of real people.

Intriguing conflicts based on today's constantly
changing life-styles.

Four new titles every month.
Available wherever paperbacks are sold.

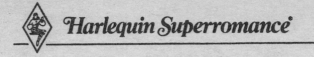

Harlequin Superromance®

CALLOWAY CORNERS

Created by four outstanding Superromance authors, bonded by lifelong friendship and a love of their home state: Sandra Canfield, Tracy Hughes, Katherine Burton and Penny Richards.

CALLOWAY CORNERS

Home of four sisters as different as the seasons, as elusive as the elements; an undiscovered part of Louisiana where time stands still and passion lasts forever.

CALLOWAY CORNERS

Birthplace of the unforgettable Calloway women: *Mariah*, free as the wind, and untamed until she meets the preacher who claims her, body and soul; *Jo*, the fiery, feisty defender of lost causes who loses her heart to a rock and roll man; *Tess*, gentle as a placid lake but tormented by her longing for the town's bad boy and *Eden*, the earth mother who's been so busy giving love she doesn't know how much she needs it until she's awakened by a drifter's kiss . . .

CALLOWAY CORNERS

Coming from Superromance, in 1989:
Mariah, by Sandra Canfield, a January release
Jo, by Tracy Hughes, a February release
Tess, by Katherine Burton, a March release
Eden, by Penny Richards, an April release